LOVE IN NAME ONLY

The Earl of Danver was duty-bound to protect his younger cousin Tom from paying with his good name for a reckless boast of amorous conquest.

Miss Sara Farthingham was bound by affection for her younger cousin Kitty to prevent the ruin of the girl's reputation after an impetuous excursion in search of adventure.

Danver and Sara had no choice but to play a game of make-believe in love to save the two young people from their folly. Danver and Sara, needless to say, were far too worldly-wise to lose their heads—and had no idea what might happen if they lost their hearts. . . .

A Choice of Cousins

A Choice of Cousins

BY APRIL KIHLSTROM

A SIGNET BOOK

NEW AMERICAN LIBRARY

TIMES MIRROR

Copyright © 1982 by April Kihlstrom

SIGNET TRADEMARK REG. U.S. PAT. OFF. AND FOREIGN COUNTRIES
REGISTERED TRADEMARK—MARCA REGISTRADA
HECHO EN CHICAGO, U.S.A.

SIGNET, SIGNET CLASSICS, MENTOR, PLUME, MERIDIAN AND NAL
BOOKS are published by The New American Library, Inc.,
1633 Broadway, New York, New York 10019

First Printing, February, 1982

1 2 3 4 5 6 7 8 9

PRINTED IN THE UNITED STATES OF AMERICA

The curricle, which drew up in front of Swinford Abbey, was clearly of a sporting design. And though the drab overcoat sported few capes, it was parted slightly to reveal a blue-and-yellow vest with a belcher neckcloth that, together, proclaimed the owner to be a member of the Four Horse Club, and hence a notable whip. Gleaming hessians, a beaver hat above dark, dishevelled locks, and buckskin pantaloons made it clear that the fellow did not altogether disdain the dictates of fashion. One would have needed, however, to see the cut of his coat to be sure. At the moment, he held the reins loosely and watched as his diminutive tiger jumped down and ran to the horses' heads. Only then did Edward Fambrough, seventh Earl of Danver, climb down, calling carelessly over his shoulder, "Take them round back, Timothy."

Ignoring the sounds that betokened compliance with his orders, Danver slowly ascended the steps to the front portal of Swinford Abbey, his ancestral home. On the third step, he paused, for a moment, to stare at the house, pulling off his gloves as he did so. The view appeared to afford him some satisfaction, for he smiled and nodded to himself. And, indeed, the Abbey was generally considered to be a most impressive sight. The original abbey had been prosperous and, due to a zealous abbot, had stubbornly held out against Henry VIII. Henry, not to be outdone, had deeded the land, and title, to the first Earl of Danver, on condition that he drive out the monks and raze the abbey to the ground. The Earl had happily done so, ignoring the curses showered on his head by the angry abbot, and used the stone to build a castle on the spot. He chose a style which could only be described as magnificent, and later earls had, from time to time, added to the structure, always maintaining the tradition of magnificence. Still, neither the current Earl, nor his father, had chosen to do more than maintain the edifice as it was.

His scrutiny completed, Danver briskly mounted the remaining steps and loudly struck the knocker against the heavy wooden door. The door was soon opened by an elderly butler, who immediately exclaimed, "My lord Danver! How gratifying to have you home again! But, may I say that we had no warning? I'm afraid your room has not been prepared!"

The Earl ignored the gentle reproof in his butler's voice and said carelessly, "Yes, yes, I daresay my arrival is rather inconvenient, but you know I shall not expect the place to be in order, Parkins. I intend to be here only a few days, and you need not even remove the holland covers from the furniture. And I promise you, I shall be satisfied with whatever food Martha manages to set before me!"

Looking a trifle harassed, as he took his master's hat, gloves, and cloak, Parkins made another attempt to explain. "That's all very well, my lord, but I fancy we can set quite an excellent dinner for you, and, sir, the furniture is already uncovered. My lady Danver," he said in an ominous tone, "is in the drawing room."

This news provoked a startled "Damn!" from the Earl. Parkins, who had his own opinion concerning the lady, was careful to avoid Danver's eyes as he added smoothly, "I understand she contemplates a long stay, sir."

"Does she?" Danver said coolly. "How unfortunate my sojourn is to be so short." Then, almost as an afterthought, he said, "My baggage will be arriving later; I'm sure you can attend to it."

"Of course, sir." Then, gently, Parkins asked, "Will you see my lady Danver now?"

Running a hand through his already disheveled locks, the Earl retorted, "Yes, yes, might as well get the curst business over with!"

Parkins bowed, then led the way to the drawing

room. It was a room the Earl thoroughly detested, furnished, as it was, with unmatched furniture, dark wine-coloured carpets, and heavy wine-coloured draperies that, even now, shut out the bright afternoon sun. Close by the fire, reclining on a couch, was a lady well past the first blush of youth, whose lace cap and modish dress announced that she had not yet meekly accepted the fact. At Danver's entrance, she drew herself upright. Pushing aside her hartshorn and vinaigrette, she held out her hands, crying, "Edward! How wonderful to see you!"

Advancing into the room, Danver took one hand, kissed it, and said, "Good day, Mother. What brings you to Swinford Abbey?"

It seemed to Danver that she looked a trifle uneasy as she said reproachfully, "My health, of course. You know how much of a trial I find the Season, particularly when there is no one at my side to support me."

The Earl ignored this gambit, merely saying, "Tell me about London, Mother."

With a languid air that disguised her eagerness, Lady Danver proceeded to relate the latest *on-dits*, interspersed with descriptions of her ailments and of complaints against members of the *ton* whom she felt had mistreated her. This gave the Earl ample time to study his parent. She did not look the part of a countess and, indeed, Edward's grandmother had made no secret of the fact that if Edward's father had not been a younger son and most unlikely to succeed to the title, the family would never have sanctioned the match. Oh, Lady Danver's birth was certainly unexceptionable, and she had not come to the marriage penniless. It was simply that Cressilia lacked the dignity expected in the wife of a Fambrough, and was irresponsible. Now, at fifty, she was as slender as ever, though her hair was beginning to show substantial streaks of grey, a circumstance not at all hidden by the youthful lace cap she wore. The colour of her dress was, as usual, purple. Lady Danver had decided, some years earlier, never to come out of half-mourning colours. They suited her light complexion admirably, and proclaimed to the world her tender devotion to her late husband's memory.

Taken altogether, Lady Danver was a delicate-looking creature who was accustomed to having her way, in spite of, or perhaps because of, her lack of inches. She almost always got what she wanted. The "almost" was important. For years, she had been trying to marry off her son to some suitable girl. Inevitably her thoughts returned to the subject now, and she paused, in mid-complaint, to regard her son. There was much to admire. The seventh Earl of Danver had a tall, powerful figure, of the sort that was displayed equally to advantage whether stripped for the ring or dressed in the most moderate of coats. To be sure, the current fashion of wearing ten or more capes on one's riding coat could only have made him appear absurd, but as Lord Danver had never aspired to the Dandy set, he bore this trial with equanimity, holding the number of his capes to four. Moreover, Danver had the compelling dark features that so many women seem to find irresistible. Or they would, she reflected, had he taken any pains to captivate any of them. But he had not, save among members of the muslin set, and *they* could not be felt to count.

Abruptly Cressilia realized that her son was politely waiting for her to continue. A sense of injustice kindling in her breast, Lady Danver said, "If you must know, Edward, the only reason I endure the Season is for *your* sake!"

Not unnaturally, this piece of intelligence staggered the Earl. He recovered quickly. "Oh? Come, now, Mother, that's doing it rather too brown."

"Well, it's so! I would be quite content to eschew the delights of the Season, did I not know that it is my duty to help you find a wife, Edward! And you must know that I never shirk my duty."

His eyes fixed on the gleam of his left boot, Danver said quietly, "Yes. I have long ago noticed that when you think of me, you invariably think in terms of duty."

As Cressilia was not a very perceptive woman, she missed the steel in her son's voice, and took the statement as a compliment. "Well, and so I do. But I quite see you are trying to turn the subject, and I won't have it! It is your duty to marry, Edward, and I cannot understand why you must be so disobliging about the matter. I am sure there are any number of amiable young ladies I have introduced you to, who would be happy to receive your addresses. Oh, Edward, I should find such comfort in having a daughter-in-law! I grow lonely in my old age."

"What? Has Henrietta left you, then?" Edward interrupted, with mock horror.

His mother regarded him with disfavour as she said, "Of course she has not, Edward! But you know very well what I mean. A companion, even if she is one's cousin, and desirous of pleasing, is not at all the same thing as a daughter-in-law and grandchildren. Oh, Edward, you know I should love grandchildren, and it is your *duty* to marry and beget an heir!"

Edward flicked an imaginary bit of dust off his sleeve as he answered carelessly, "Oh, but there is young Haverstock, you know."

"That is *not* the same thing!" his mother replied severely. "Your duty—"

Ruthlessly Danver cut her off, "Ah, but you must know, Mother, that I am not at all concerned with duty. I leave *that* to you!"

For a moment the lady was silenced. Then, undaunted, she went on, "You are just like your father, Edward. He had no thought for his duty, or for my comfort. But I am not one to complain, I—"

Again Danver cut his mother off. "How fortunate," he said in a grim voice, "for you must know I should tolerate no criticism of my father."

Immediately Lady Danver was all contrition. "Of course not, Edward!"

Whatever else Lady Danver might have said went unspoken as the drawing room door opened and a woman of uncertain age entered, a silk Norwich shawl draped over one arm. As she entered, she said, "Here is your shawl, Cressy. I do hope it is the one you wish. Oh! Edward! I did not see you! How nice to have you here!"

Danver walked forward to greet her, saying, "Hullo, Henny. How do you go on?" Henrietta Ramsey looked up at the Earl towering over her, and smiled tremulously as he added, "Are you quite comfortable here?"

Henrietta felt a trifle overcome by the Earl's attention. She was one of those spinsters of middle age who, having no real alternative, place themselves at the disposal of more solvent relatives. She was, Danver knew, some sort of distant cousin of his mother, and had come to Swinford Abbey to help out at the time of the sixth Earl's death. Edward could not forget her calm good sense when everyone else had been so distraught, and was pleased that she had chosen to stay on with his mother. For some unfathomable reason, both ladies were eminently satisfied with the arrangement. Now Henrietta blushed as she said, "Oh, so very comfortable! But then, we always are, here at Swinford Abbey. Your servants are so well trained, and the house so . . . so . . ."

"Magnificent?" Danver hazarded. "I should not call that a recommendation. For my part, I sometimes think I should prefer to trade the magnificence for a neat little manor, with proper hallways, and no drafts, without miles to walk from my bedchamber to the dining rooms."

"Edward! You cannot mean that!" his mother said sharply, reminding the others of her presence.

Danver shrugged, but Henrietta said, gently shaking her head at him, "I might believe you, did I not know how much time and concern you devote to the estate. Mr. Bowen tells me you are far more accessible than your father ever was."

As the sixth Earl of Danver had shown no interest whatsoever in learning about the estate, this was hardly an overwhelming compliment. But, in fact, Edward did spend a great deal of time overseeing his lands. Unlike his father, he *had* expected to be the Earl someday, and had always taken seriously the responsibilities that would accompany the position. Now, a gleam in his eye, Danver grinned down at Henny and said, so softly that his mother could not hear, "So Mr. Bowen discusses my affairs with you, does he, Henny? Now, I wonder what that could mean? Am I to wish you happy?"

For a moment her mischievous smile matched his; then she was serious again, and shook her head, replying as softly, "Not yet."

Lady Danver had not heard the exchange of words, but she had caught the reference to the bailiff. Imperiously she said, "Come here, Henny, and bring me my shawl. I hope this mention of Mr. Bowen does not mean you have forgotten yourself so far as to gossip with the servants!"

Draping the shawl around Lady Danver's shoulders, Henrietta replied soothingly, "No, no, of course not! Why, a fine thing that should be!" Then, wishing to escape further questions from her ladyship, Henrietta asked the Earl, "Are you here to inspect the estate, my lord?"

Danver nodded, amused. "Yes. That, and to escape the start of the Season. I thought anything preferable to the boredom attendant upon watching a bunch of silly chits take their place in Society."

"Ah, you realized that Swinford Abbey would be just the thing, for excitement?" Henrietta said with an air of reflection.

Danver laughed. "Yes, well, but I shall be returning to London in a few days, and no doubt shall quickly recover from the gaiety of Yorkshire, and Swinford Abbey."

"Yorkshire!" Lady Danver exclaimed. "Is that where you've been? Not a repairing lease, I hope? Although how anyone, on so generous an income as yours, could possibly outrun the tailor, is beyond me!"

The Earl smiled wryly. "No, Mother, *not* a repairing lease. Webberly thought he might wish to sell his matching chestnuts, and I went with him to Yorkshire to see if I might wish to buy them. Devilish fine horseflesh," Danver added reflectively, "but Webberly decided to keep them, after all. Took three weeks to make up his mind."

"His father was the same," Lady Danver said with some complacence. "*He* could never make up his mind, either. He spent two months deciding to propose, and in the end, your father asked me first. Not that I should have accepted Webberly, he was shockingly tight-fisted in those days. Still is, from what I hear."

"Why? Did he refuse to frank you at loo?" Danver asked quizzingly. When this only produced an icy glare from his mother, Danver went on soothingly,

"Never mind. Tell me, Mother, did you see Tom while you were in London?"

Lady Danver answered a trifle pettishly, "I am sure we must have been, more than once, at the same affair, but they were shocking squeezes and I am sure it is not wonderful that he should prefer to dance attendance on girls his own age, rather than on me. Nor would Haverstock ever think to call and pay his respects." She hesitated, then added, "Perhaps you should know, Edward, since you are one of his guardians, that he has been showing a remarkable interest in some chit just out."

Danver shrugged. "An infatuation will do him no harm."

"Yes, but I am not sure it is an infatuation," Lady Danver persisted, "particularly on her part. She seems a scheming girl, to me, and she must know Tom is your heir. I should not be at all surprised to learn that she has hopes of becoming a countess!"

Knowing that his mother's concern sprang more from the fear that Haverstock would marry before Danver, than from worry over Tom's happiness, Danver answered lightly, "Ah, but you forget that I stand in the way. And I might be expected to marry, myself, someday."

With some asperity, Lady Danver retorted, "Yes, if you hadn't convinced everyone you were a hopeless case!"

Hastily Henrietta intervened, saying, "No doubt Edward will see the girl in London, and can decide for himself."

Danver nodded. "As you say, I shall see for myself.

And now, Mother, I must leave you and go look over the accounts."

Lady Danver nodded graciously, and Henny gave Danver a friendly smile, so that the Earl was able to make good his escape. Once free of the drawing room, he immediately made his way to the library. This was one of the few truly comfortable rooms at Swinford Abbey. Although it was panelled in the same dark wood as his mother's drawing room, Danver's library was far brighter, for he had had it furnished in blues and golds, and his first action, upon entering, was to throw back the curtains to let in the light. A fire had already been laid in the fireplace, and Danver knelt to set it alight. He should, of course, have summoned a servant for the task, but he had less concern for his dignity than they did. Finally, Danver turned to the massive oak desk and took out the current account ledger. He did not, however, open it. His thoughts were too full of the recent conversation with his mother, and with Henny. It was true that Danver's friends considered him resolutely opposed to marriage; his own, at any rate. In his cups, he had even been known to declare that a man was a fool to give up his freedom for some selfish, demanding female and a parcel of brats.

In recent years, the Earl had curbed his tongue, and such indiscreet comments no longer came from him. But his behaviour was such as to lead all, save a few incurably optimistic mamas, to feel that his sentiments had undergone no change. Danver, himself, was conscious of no emptiness in his life. He had any

number of male friends, and there were several
ladies, who inhabited a certain stratum, that had not
been unkind. And although Danver was very much
aware of his duty to provide an heir, he felt that, at
nine-and-twenty, he still had a great deal of time before he need do so. Particularly in view of the exis-
tence of his cousin, and ward, Tom Haverstock, who
stood next in line for the title. He was, in fact, quite
fond of the boy. Indeed, being a rather amiable fellow beneath his quelling exterior, Danver had spent
a number of hours demonstrating to Tom his particular method of arranging a neckcloth in the style he
had created. It was known as the Willow, and an
ability to imitate his cousin's arrangement had
greatly enhanced young Haverstock's credit among
his friends.

So, had he been asked, Danver would have been at
a loss to say what made him pause over the matter
now. Unless, perhaps, it had been the look in
Henny's eyes when she had spoken of his bailiff, Mr.
Bowen.

Abruptly the Earl flipped open the ledger, determined to shake off the unaccustomed mood. Fortunately, he was quickly able to fulfill this resolve,
becoming so engrossed that Parkins was finally
forced to interrupt and inform Danver that he
would have to hurry if he was to have time to dress
before supper.

2

It was, in the end, several mornings later than he had expected, when the Earl of Danver arrived at his London town house. Since he had sent the greater part of his baggage, and his valet, ahead the night before, the house stood perfectly ready to receive the Earl. James, Danver's butler, expressed himself gratified to have the master home again. Danver, shedding his coat, hat, and gloves, retorted, "Are you? How can you be, when you know I shall turn the place upside down!"

James permitted himself to smile at this pleasantry, and said, "I cannot imagine my lord doing so. However, I can assure you, none of the staff would have the least objection if you did so."

Danver laughed and accepted the information that the mail, which had come in his absence, lay on his

15

desk in the library. In addition, there was a gratifying number of cards, which had been left by callers
in the last week, on the salver in the hall. The Earl
glanced through these carelessly and was surprised to
find that Tom had apparently called every day. He
turned to James, who stood waiting unobtrusively.
Casually Danver asked, "At what time of day has my
cousin Haverstock been in the habit of calling?"

"Early afternoon, sir."

Danver nodded, hesitated, then said, "That will
be all for now, James."

"Very good, sir."

The Earl strode down the hallway to his library.
That room, though smaller than the one at Swinford
Abbey, was a very pleasant one. Cream curtains were
pulled back to allow in the daylight, and blue-and-
cream carpets were scattered about the floor, allowing polished wood to show between them. The
panelling was lighter, and the furniture more delicate, than at the Abbey. Danver was not surprised to
find that his secretary had been busy, in his absence,
preparing correspondence and noting political
speeches that might interest his lordship. For Danver, upon inheriting the title, had taken his seat in
Parliament. To be sure, he was not an overly political man, but he was also not a man to shirk his responsibilities. Employing an industrious secretary,
who could be counted upon to follow (and inform
Danver of) all important political events, was perhaps a compromise between duty and comfort. It
really answered very well. Danver settled down for
an hour's work or so before luncheon.

The Earl was just on the point of rising from this luncheon, when Tom was ushered in. Danver smiled broadly, holding out a hand, as he said, "Tom! Good to see you. It's about time I returned to London, for I see you have forgotten how to tie your neckcloth!"

Young Haverstock grasped Danver's hand, flushing, torn between defiance and pleasure, as he retorted, "No such thing! I've abandoned the Willow for the Waterfall."

Danver regarded the neckcloth in question before saying, "Is that what it's called? I should have called it the *Bizarre*."

"Stop roasting me, Ned!" Tom retorted, without rancour. Then he added, "I must say, it's devilish good to see you again!"

"And you," Danver replied, and indicating the table, said, "Will you join me?"

Having the usual excellent appetite of a young man of eighteen, Tom readily fell in with this suggestion, and the footman was quick to set a place for him. Danver let Tom eat in silence, content to study his cousin. There was much to please and nothing, save perhaps the neckcloth, to offend, in the young man's appearance. He was of moderate height, with a trim figure and a neat leg. If his shirt points were high, they were not excessively so, and though the Earl would have wagered that it took two men to ease Tom into his coat, it lacked the padded shoulders and pinched waist that many men affected. And if Tom was overly fond of rings and fobs and such, at least they were all in excellent taste. Nor could one have found fault with the burnished gold locks arranged *coup du vent*, the yellow pantaloons, or in the gleaming hessians Tom sported. In short, Haverstock was a very creditable young man.

It was not until Tom appeared to be ending his meal that Danver spoke. "Tell me, Tom. Have you any notion why my mother has chosen to retire to Swinford Abbey?" When it became clear that Tom was reluctant to speak, Danver frowned. "As bad as that? Come, you may as well tell me."

"There was talk of her health, but . . ." Tom began.

"But she seemed in excellent sorts?" the Earl offered. "Are you sure she did not confide in your mother?"

Tom reddened. "There may have been gambling debts."

"I see. So she was badly dipped again. Go on, I feel sure she said more than that to your mother."

Tom hesitated; then anger got the better of him. "Dash it, it's the outside of enough! She told my mother she'd have been able to come about if you only gave her a decent allowance. Called you clutch-fisted. You! I wish I may see it."

Danver's face grew a trifle grim. "Indeed? Well, so I am, with her. I've told my mother she may spend as much of her own money as she chooses, but that I shall not frank her gaming. Good Lord, her portion was perfectly respectable!"

"Though nothing like your own," Tom pointed out.

The Earl's eyes were hard as he said, "That was my father's choice." A moment later, the tension in his shoulders eased, and he said easily, "Well, no wonder my mother chose not to confide in me. Have you any other news?"

To Danver's surprise, Tom hesitated, turned a deep red, and said, "I'm going to be married, Ned. I'm sorry if you don't like it, but I love her!"

The Earl surveyed his cousin through his glass. "Strange!" he murmured at last. "You don't look deranged." Then, louder, "I see. When is the wedding to be? And, I realize this is a mere quibble, Tom, but I don't recall seeing a notice in the *Gazette*, or the *Morning Post*."

Tom flushed again. "Damme! You know very well I'm underage, Ned. Can't do anything without your consent. Or her parents' consent."

Danver smiled. "I see. I collect *they* don't know of this, either. Tell me. Who, besides yourself, does know?"

"My mother," Haverstock replied defensively. "And, of course, Kitty. At least, that is, she knows how I feel about her. Her parents aren't in town, so I haven't spoken with her father, but her aunt, who is bringing Kitty out, likes me."

"I'm quite sure she does," Danver observed obscurely. Then, "Has this paragon, er, Kitty, a last name?"

"Of course she does!" Tom retorted indignantly. "Farthingham! It's a very respectable family."

"To be sure," Danver murmured. Aloud he said, "Do you know, Tom, I almost wish you had taken up with an opera dancer instead? Then I should have known what to do."

"Do? What have you to do, but meet Kitty and give your consent?" Tom demanded. "If you refuse, it don't really signify, you know. I fancy my mother's consent would be enough and, what's more, she'd give it, too!"

The Earl, who was well acquainted with the lady, and had no great opinion of her understanding, was inclined to agree. Casually he said, "Yes, but *I* hold the purse strings, for a few years, yet, and if I dislike the marriage, I can close them."

Shocked, Tom cried, "Ned! You wouldn't?"

"Give me time," Danver said wryly, "before I answer you. Recollect that I have not yet met the girl, and that I consider you rather young to be leg-shackled."

"No such thing!" Tom protested. "*Your* father was my age when *he* married!"

"Precisely."

That silenced Tom. Several moments later, however, he said, "Well, I never thought you'd behave so shabbily, Ned. But it's only because you haven't met Kitty. Come with me now, and I'll introduce you."

Danver raised an eyebrow, saying languidly, "Indeed? I am sorry I cannot oblige you, Tom, but I have other commitments. You may present me some other time."

Tom, whose face had begun to cloud at Danver's first words, brightened at this, and said, "Of course. As long as it is soon!"

"It shall be, it shall be," the Earl promised. Then, easily, "By the way, Tom. Tell me, how long have you known the young lady? Is the attachment of long standing?"

"Oh, yes!" Tom replied blithely. "Kitty, Miss Farthingham, has been in London since the very start of the Season, and I knew at once how I felt. I can assure you, Ned, this is not a passing fancy."

Only a strong affection for his cousin kept Danver from pointing out that he would have felt more at ease if it had been a passing fancy. It was possible, of course, that the attachment was a deep one, and that the lady was unexceptionable. In that event, Danver would be inclined to give his consent, in spite of Tom's age. The question was, was the lady acceptable? Tom had, up till now, shown a regrettable predilection for vulgar company and, only one year before, become enamoured of a bit of fluff, not realizing she was not a 'lady. The Earl had been hard put to nip that one in the bud, as the young woman in question had been very clever. It was true that Lady 'Danver had said that this one was a chit just out, but that did not ensure that Miss Farthingham was suitable for Tom. Lady Danver had also said she was odiously scheming. None of this showed, however, on Danver's face as he said, "Well, we shall see."

Tom nodded, knowing it was useless to push his cousin on the issue. Instead, he said naively, "You will excuse me now, won't you, Ned? Kitty don't like to be kept waiting."

Lazily the Earl waved him away. "I quite understand," he said.

"Knew you would!" was the enthusiastic reply.

Lord Danver's first order of business, once Tom was gone, was to call on a certain lady residing in St. John's Wood. She had been accommodating, diverting, and even rather intelligent. Danver was at a loss, therefore, to explain to himself why he had decided to take final leave of her; he only knew that she no longer interested him. Reluctantly he ordered his phaeton brought round.

Sometime later, the Earl could be seen ascending the steps of the lady's house. He was admitted without delay, and the interview went much as expected. Both parties were well aware that the lady's heart was untouched and that the Earl had been, and now was, generous. This did not prevent the lady from making an unpleasant scene, which was only to be expected from one who had once trod the boards. In any event, it was an angry Earl who emerged from the house and signalled his tiger to hand him the reins. Rather grimly Danver said, "Hold tight, Timothy. I plan to spring 'em!"

Timothy, having seen his master's face, had no need of the warning; indeed, he expected worse. But they were in London, after all, and there were limits to the recklessness one could engage in. This was, perhaps, unfortunate, for Danver's rage had scarcely abated when he espied his cousin Tom with a young woman. She was tall, as tall as Tom, with soft brown curls crowned by a poke bonnet. She wore a modish green walking dress that displayed her slender figure to advantage, and her hand was tucked, confidingly, into Tom's arm. And she was laughing at something he said. Tom, meanwhile, gave her hand a squeeze, and gazed at her with blatant admiration. The Earl could cheerfully have wrung her neck. It was clear, to his experienced eye, that she was older than his cousin, by several years, and only a harpy, Danver felt, would so ensnare a boy younger than herself.

As the Earl watched, Tom let go of the lady's hand, and she entered a rather fashionable establishment. Tom then continued up the street. To Timothy's surprise, Danver made no attempt to hail his ward, but continued driving in the opposite direction.

When the young lady emerged from the milliner's shop, Danver was waiting. "Miss Farthingham?"

The young woman looked at Danver with some surprise. A slight blush stealing over her features, she said, "Yes?"

"I am Lord Danver, Tom Haverstock's cousin. May I escort you home?"

Miss Sara Farthingham barely glanced at the waiting phaeton, or the card Danver handed her as proof of his identity. From the cool tone of her voice, no one would have guessed the tumult in Sara's breast as she said impulsively, "Why?"

Taken aback, Danver answered, without pausing to reflect, "I wish to speak with you."

It was Sara's turn to be startled. Propriety spoke against accepting his escort, but something else, perhaps curiosity, prompted her to say, "Very well, my lord."

Danver gave a slight bow, then handed Miss Farthingham into his phaeton. Up close, he found her very attractive, with large brown eyes that met his enquiringly. Danver decided that she must be very sure of her hold over Tom, to meet him so calmly. The Earl was determined she would regret her over-confidence. To his tiger he said, "You may return home, Timothy. Stand away from their heads!"

Timothy had no chance to protest, and began the walk home, grumbling, and wondering if his master had a touch of fever.

Sara was wondering the same thing. After endur-ing several minutes of grim silence, she said gently, "You wished to speak with me, my lord?"

That broke the trance and Danver said bluntly, "Yes. Tom Haverstock. You are well acquainted with him, I believe?"

"Why, yes, of course." Sara smiled. "We see him quite often. A delightful boy!"

The Earl smiled also, a trifle grimly. "So you think of him as a boy, do you? Are you aware of his age?"

Puzzled, Sara replied, "Eighteen, I should guess."

"You are correct. May I venture to suppose that *you*, Miss Farthingham, are rather older?"

"By three years," she said frankly.

Scornfully Danver laughed. "I wonder you are not ashamed to admit it! Or is your position so secure with Tom that you feel you need no longer take care? Tell me, do you make a practice of enslaving young boys?"

For a moment Sara was certain that the Earl of Danver had gone mad. Then gradually the truth came to her: Lord Danver had mistaken Sara (how?) for Kitty. Close upon this came the realization that he must have seen her with Tom earlier. Her first impulse was to inform Lord Danver of his mistake; her second impulse was to teach him a lesson, for she could not but find his high-handed manner offensive. Both impulses warred until, taking her silence for chagrin, Danver said, "Will you let him go? You must have older, more suitable admirers."

In a voice she fought to keep soft, Sara said, "I do not see what affair this is of yours."

"I hold the purse strings!" Danver answered contemptuously. "You didn't know that, did you? His mother and I are joint guardians, except in financial matters, where I have full control. And, I assure you, I will not countenance so ill-conceived a match! Surely you can not want him? A mere boy! I've no doubt you could aim higher, if you chose. I might even help you."

This was too much for Sara. Anger drowned all common sense, and she retorted, "How kind of you! But I think I find the idea too uncertain. In any event, I shall do as I please about Tom."

"Shall you?" The Earl's voice was dangerously grim. "Allow me to say that you are being very foolish."

Choking with fury, Sara retorted, "And allow me to say that I find you excessively ill-bred! I wager that it is you, and not I, who will regret today's words!"

"Pretty words, but I take leave to doubt it!" Then, "Your house, Miss Farthingham. You will pardon me, I know, but I cannot leave the horses to escort you in."

Unassisted, Sara scrambled down, grateful no one

was about to witness her anger. Resolutely turning her back on the Earl, she climbed the steps as Danver drove away. Sara distinctly heard him say, "Jade!"

Somehow she made it through the front door. Then, alone in the alcove, she stood clenching and unclenching her fists. At that moment, Sara would have given anything to be a man, so that she could have thrashed the Earl as he deserved. No matter that his rude words had sprung from a mistaken notion of her identity; such behaviour was not to be tolerated!

A few minutes later, her hat and gloves discarded, Sara stood in the doorway of the Yellow Saloon. Only Kitty was there, poring over the latest dress patterns. It was evident that she had not witnessed Sara's arrival, for she looked up in surprise and asked, "Back already? Is Tom with you?"

"No"—Sara shook her head—"he had errands of his own to run." Then, studying her cousin, Sara smiled. Kitty was fair, with glowing cheeks, riotous blond curls, and sparkling green eyes. The dress she wore was a sprigged-muslin confection that set her petite figure off to perfection. In short, she was enchanting. Impulsively Sara said, "Well, if you will go about looking so lovely, it's no wonder everyone falls in love with you!"

As Kitty laughed, dimples appeared. "Not quite everyone." She tossed her head. "Tom fears his guardian may disapprove of me."

"Kitty! Tom never said so?" Sara demanded.

"Well, he did," Kitty assured her cousin. "But it don't signify. I've no intention of marrying Tom."

Staring at her hands, Sara said, "Tom seems very particular in his attentions."

Kitty gave a scornful gurgle of laughter. "Of course he is! He fancies himself in love with me, doesn't he? But it wouldn't answer, you know," she concluded loftily. "He is far too young."

This, coming from Kitty, who was barely seventeen, was too much for Sara. Laughing, she said, "I see. And you are so very old, of course, that it would never do!"

"Sara, stop roasting me!" Kitty stamped her foot. "You know very well what I mean! A girl of eighteen or twenty is ready for marriage, but a man ought to be at least twenty-five."

Uneasiness stirred in Sara, as she wondered just *whom* Kitty might be thinking of, but she kept her voice light as she said, "Perhaps you ought to aim for the guardian, then. I understand he is even an earl."

"Oh, no," Kitty answered pragmatically. "He would surely be far too old, and I have no intention of marrying anyone over thirty."

Again, uneasiness stirred, for this was the first time Sara had heard Kitty set limits to her ambition, but she only said, "He isn't over thirty."

"Now you are roasting me again," Kitty accused. "How could he possibly be Tom's guardian, if he is as young as you say?"

Sara was not required to answer, for at that moment Adele Farthingham entered the Yellow Saloon. She was dressed, as always, in the kick of fashion. A

pale lavender dress of crape favoured her fair colouring, and she moved with a charming air of helpless-
ness. An outsider, seeing the three ladies, would
have instantly concluded that Adele and Kitty were
mother and daughter, so alike did they look. Sara,
taking after her tall, dark father, was decidedly the
odd one out. Both Farthingham men, however, had
married women who looked very much alike, hence
the resemblance between aunt and niece. Adele
greeted Sara and Kitty affectionately, and added,
"Who were you talking about?"

"Tom," Kitty replied promptly. "Sara says that his
guardian, the Earl of Danver, is not above thirty."

Taking a seat, Adele nodded. "It was considered
quite eccentric of the older Haverstock. He neglect-
ed to specify *which* Earl of Danver was to have the
guardianship. Which was shockingly careless of him,
I must say, particularly as the present Earl's father
died more than six months before Haverstock, so
that there was time enough to alter the will, had he
taken the trouble to do so! Naturally, everyone considered it quite absurd that Danver, at twenty-five,
should have guardianship of a boy of fourteen. Nevertheless, the will held, and I believe Danver is said
to have managed the business tolerably well." Adele
paused, and then added, "I have even heard it said
that the elder Haverstock was not fond of his only
son."

"You mean his father might not have cared who
had the guardianship?" Sara was frankly appalled.

Adele chose her words carefully. "I believe Tom's
father was an avid sportsman and Tom rather unin-

terested in hunting and such. Perhaps he felt that both the old Earl and his son would be capable of molding Tom to the proper pattern."

Sara could not but feel a certain sympathy for Tom, her own parents having never ceased to try to pattern *her* after her mother. Kitty, however, was becoming bored with the business, and demanded, "Who cares? Have you ever met the Earl?"

"I have seen him. He is well enough to look at, and his manners, when he chooses, can be quite charming. But he is generally considered not to be a marrying man," Adele answered respressively.

Kitty turned to Sara, not at all abashed. "Have you met him, Sara?"

Sara considered, and discarded, the notion of telling Kitty about her recent encounter. Instead, carelessly, she said, "Oh, yes. In my first Season, I even danced with him, at Almack's, once or twice."

Kitty immediately pounced on this. "Did you? What was he like? Tell me!"

Sara barely hesitated. "Lord Danver is quite tall, well-built, with broad shoulders. His features are pleasing, if rather rough, and his hair dark. He might be handsome if he smiled, but a slight frown is his habitual expression. Moreover, Danver is always well-dressed, but inclined more to comfort than to the first stare of fashion."

Kitty stared at her cousin, amazed. "Why, you speak as if you had just seen him!" As Sara flushed, Kitty laughed. "Sara! Had you a *tendre* for him? Does he remember you, as well?"

Annoyed, Sara said tartly, "Nonsense! I consider

Danver quite odious. And I daresay that if he were to see me, today, he would have no notion he had ever met me before. Recollect that that was three years ago, and these past two years we have been in mourning for Papa."

Disappointed, Kitty said, "Oh, well. But you are going about now, and perhaps this year you will take!"

At this point, Adele interrupted, saying sadly, "I have always thought it a pity, Sara, that you could not bring yourself to accept Mr. Dockhurst."

With quiet emphasis Sara replied, "I would rather be an ape-leader, Mama, than marry where there is not the least affection. Nor," she added frankly, "should I care to be a stepmother, at my age. Particularly to a girl barely five years my junior. Depend upon it, she would resent me, and how could I blame her?"

"Think of it!" Kitty said in awed tones. "In two years, you should be obliged to bring her out!"

"That will do!" Adele said a trifle sharply. Then, wistfully, "If only, Sara, you could contrive to lose your shyness!"

"It is not shyness," Sara corrected her mother gently. "It is simply that I don't choose to put myself forward."

"Forward?" Kitty demanded. "I suppose next you will say that *I* am fast!"

Adele Farthingham, in ignorance of certain of Kitty's recent activities, hastened to reassure her, "No, no, my love. Depend upon it, some might envy your success, but no one could call you bold!"

Adele was wrong, however. Lord Danver not only called her bold, he decided she was graceless and lacking in conscience, as well. For a tuppence, he would have wrung her neck, but settled for mangling his gloves, instead. It was in this amiable mood that he arrived at White's. Two of his particular friends, Sir Frederick Tiverton and Mr. Anthony Baffington, immediately espied him. "Ned! Good to see you! But you're a week late. Baffy expected you two nights ago for his card party."

"Freddy! How do you go on? Yes, I know I'm late. Webberly took forever to decide about his cattle, and then I stopped home to check on the estate. But I shan't say I'm sorry, for you know I find the Season a dead bore," Danver said, greeting his friend.

"No, no!" Mr. Baffington protested. "That's coming it too strong. Don't much take to doing the pretty, to the ladies, myself, but the parties ain't a bore. Lord, you'll never find fellows playing so strong, or so deep, as during the Season."

Danver laughed. "Oh, aye, Baffy, we all know what a gamester you are! But Freddy and I are neither as skilled nor as lucky as you, and should soon find ourselves badly dipped if we played neck or nothing, as you do."

Baffington, who was well aware of the Earl's skill, at cards and otherwise, merely snorted and asked, "New coat? Weston, I'll wager. Wish he'd make me some like yours, but he always insists I haven't the figure for it. Dashed if I understand the fellow!"

Danver's eyes danced at this, but he managed to preserve his countenance and reply soothingly, "Perhaps he wishes to emphasize your, er, resemblance to the Regent."

This reference to Baffington's considerable girth caused the fellow to frown as he turned the notion over in his mind. Finally he said, "Well, if he thinks I'll take to wearing stays, he's much mistaken the matter, for I tell you frankly, I won't. Dashed things creak!"

This was too much for his friends, who burst out laughing. Baffy became alarmed, protesting, "Here! I say! It's no laughing matter. How could I concentrate on my cards, if the damme thing began creaking on me?"

Not unnaturally, this only produced further laughter. It was Tiverton who finally managed to reply, "Don't worry, Baffy. If Weston tries to make you wear a corset, you need only threaten to take your business to Stultz!"

Baffy was much pleased with the notion. "Why, so I could! Obliged to you, Freddy, though I hope I shan't have to," he confided. "Much prefer Weston."

Judging it expeditious to change the subject, Danver asked his friends, "Did you see the mill at Crossbridge? I hear they went twenty rounds."

Tiverton laughed. "They went twenty rounds, all right, but not out of skill, rather from the lack of it!"

"Silliest thing I ever saw," Baffy confirmed. "Neither even managed to draw the other's cork!"

Danver raised an eyebrow. "However did they manage to end it, then?" he asked.

Tiverton shrugged. "The Young'un planted a

facer, and it turned out that the Red had a glass chin. Went right down. Lord, Jackson said he'd never allow either one *near* his Saloon."

For a time, the talk was of boxing and other gentlemanly sports, but eventually even this topic was exhausted. It was then that Danver broached the subject of his concern.

"The Farthingham chit?" Freddy asked. "You must mean the girl your ward is acting the moon calf over. Lord, you should have seen his face when he found I had claimed her first waltz at Almack's!"

"So she has vouchers for Almack's, eh?" There was a quizzical gleam in Danver's eyes. "I gather, then, that she moves in the best circles? But you, Freddy? Are you smitten, also?"

"Can't be," Baffy asserted bluntly. "Mind you, I don't say she ain't taking, for she is, but she's helpless as a kitten! Almost as mindless as one, too. Now, I ask you, is Freddy the man to be attracted by such a chit? 'Course not! Bamming you if he says he is."

Danver looked distinctly puzzled. "*Kitten*, you say? Are you sure you don't mean *cat*?"

Tiverton laughed self-consciously. "She's a beauty, Ned, and completely artless. A man finds himself wanting to take care of her. I don't much fancy the role, but there are a good many who do. And the chit's aunt is determined to bring someone, anyone, but preferably a title and wealth, up to scratch. Someone ought to warn young Haverstock, but boys of that age are totally heedless."

"Wrong thing to do, anyway," Baffy offered. "Ten

to one, it would only set his back up, and he would offer for her!"

"You forget I should have something to say to that," Danver retorted grimly.

"Don't say yes, don't say no," Baffy countered, "but if he did contrive a runaway marriage, would you tie shut the purse strings? 'Course not! Scandal, you know."

"He has more sense than to fly to the border!" Danver said, relaxing a little. "And if she has as many admirers as you say, she may not even choose to accept my ward."

Both Baffy and Tiverton felt this to be a wise observation, and it was voted time to go in to dinner.

The conversation had not, however, relieved Danver's fears. Instead, he found himself deeply puzzled. That Miss Farthingham might contrive to fool a green youth, such as Tom, he did not doubt. But Baffy and Tiverton were a far different matter. Both had entered their thirtieth year safely single, and were accustomed to seeing pretty young misses. No, if anything, Danver's uneasiness had grown upon hearing his friends describe Miss Farthingham.

Perhaps that was why he was so pleased to see Tom the next morning and to have the chance to ask him, "Tell me, Tom. Is there, by chance, more than one Miss Farthingham?"

"Oh, yes!" Tom answered blithely, confirming Danver's fears. "There's Kitty's cousin, Sara Farthingham. Why?"

"I just wondered," Danver said grimly, carving a

slice of ham for Tom, as he added, "Tell me, is she very tall, with brown hair?"

"Quite. Just the opposite of Kitty," Tom replied, taking the plate from his cousin. "She's rather older than Kitty, and well enough to look at, but rather too in control of herself for a fellow's comfort, if you understand what I mean," he added carelessly.

Tom paused, and Danver said, "I do."

Given this encouragement, Tom went on, "Not that I mean to say she's an antidote. Not by a long way. She can be great fun, as well as give a fellow good advice, at times."

"Good God!" Danver exclaimed involuntarily. "Do you mean to say she's coached you with her cousin?"

"No, no, Ned! As if I should let her! I only meant she has a way of helping a fellow see things sensibly. Well, when Kitty chose to waltz with your friend Tiverton, I was within an ace of walking out of Almack's. It was Sara who explained it wouldn't have been the thing for Kitty to dance with me more than twice. Blister it, how would I have known, if she hadn't told me?"

With difficulty, Danver kept his countenance. "I see. And, er, did you leave?"

" 'Course not!" Tom's voice was scornful. "Should have made a cake of myself, if I had. Sara had a better idea. Suggested I ask other young ladies to dance. Throw dust in the eyes of all the spiteful old tabbies who were watching us. Not that Sara used quite those words," Tom added conscientiously. "But it was a devilish good notion, don't you think?"

"Very wise," Danver agreed gravely, beginning to think that Miss Sara Farthingham was a young woman of rare good sense. This impression was shattered by Tom's next statement.

"She knows *you*, Ned. Sara, I mean. Must have seen you at Almack's, or some place, where you were high in the instep. Did a marvelous imitation of you playing off your rank, once, when we were alone and I had told her you were my cousin." Tom chuckled at the memory. "Lord, if she weren't a lady, I'd wager she could make her fortune on the stage!"

The Earl was anything but gratified to receive this intelligence. "I see," he said grimly. "I gather Miss Sara Farthingham is much given to impersonations?"

Realizing he had said something wrong, Tom tried to make amends. "You needn't worry, Ned! She's very discreet about it. Knows it could land her in the boughs if the wrong person saw her. Especially if they saw her doing someone like Byron. Sara don't like him overmuch, you know."

"No, I don't know." Danver bit off the words. "I gather Sara dislikes rather everyone?"

"No, no, you've quite mistaken the matter!" Tom cried. "Sara *likes* most everyone. It's only those people who she believes think too much of themselves, that she can't abide. In general, she is at great pains to put one at one's ease, and I have seen her go out of her way to be nice to someone or other."

"I see. And I am one of the ones she finds too haughty?" Danver asked.

"That's because she don't know you, Ned," Tom said, eager to explain. "Daresay, if I introduced you,

you'd get along famously. Why don't you come to my mother's party tonight? Bound to meet both of them there."

"I'll be there. I expect to have a great deal to say to Miss Sara Farthingham!" Danver answered feelingly.

After Tom had gone, the Earl retreated to his library and savoured visions of strangling Miss Sara Farthingham. Lord Danver was well aware of his consequence, but never before had anyone had the temerity to suggest he was arrogant. The charge pained him for it was the last thing he would have chosen to have anyone think of him. Reflection, however, and an innate honesty, forced Danver to admit that he might well have given that impression, at times. Further reflection informed him that his behaviour the day before could only have confirmed Miss Farthingham in her disgust of him. Although he had mistaken the young lady's identity, and she ought to have informed him of his error, Danver could not but admit that his words had been unforgiveable.

Not unnaturally, this all served to increase the Earl's anger. He made a private vow that the next time he should encounter Miss Sara Farthingham, she should find nothing in his conduct to censure. Having formed this admirable resolution, Danver turned to the papers on his desk, and tried to forget her.

3

Sara Farthingham dressed with great care for Lady Haverstock's ball. Her gown was of an unusual shade of green, over a white satin slip, with tiny puff sleeves and lace trim. There were satin slippers to match, and long gloves of the same unusual sea-green. All of this was Sara's own choice, for now that Adele Farthingham had an accredited beauty to dress, she was content to give Sara her head. This was a fortunate circumstance, for although Lady Farthingham knew precisely how to turn out a *blonde* beauty, she lacked an eye for what would suit one of Sara's unusual build and colouring. And Sara could not but be grateful that her age precluded the necessity to dress in the insipid colours decreed suitable for a girl's first Season. A dress of sea-green became her far better.

Kitty, of course, wore white, but her gown was of gauze shot with silver threads. She was ravishing, from the knot of curls on her head, to the delicate feet encased in white satin slippers. And as Sara entered Kitty's room, her maid fastened a small circlet of pearls about Kitty's neck. That they suited her perfectly did not prevent Kitty from complaining that she would rather have had Sara's delicate emeralds instead. "Should you?" Sara asked with some amusement. "*I* think they should spoil the impression you give one, of being a sort of fairy princess."

Kitty studied her reflection in the glass and sighed. "I suppose you are right. But, Sara, I should never have known you, you look so . . . so . . ."

"Pretty?" the maid suggested.

Sara chuckled. "Thank you! I think I may know how to take that! So I am usually an antidote, am I? No, no, it's all right, I haven't taken offense. I understand what you mean. Tonight, I'm no longer the drab little mouse, is that it?"

Both maid and mistress nodded. After a moment, Kitty said, "It's not just the dress, though I think it vastly becoming and wonder when you can have ordered it, but perhaps it's that you look as though you expect to enjoy yourself!"

Sara laughed, again, at the surprise in Kitty's voice. "Well, perhaps I do. Is that so strange?"

From the expression on Kitty's face, it seemed she thought so, but she had no chance to speak, for Adele Farthingham came in, saying, "Come along, my loves. We're already fashionably late. Have you your gloves? Reticules? Shawls? Good! Then let us be off!"

Quite happily the two girls followed Adele down the stairs and out to the carriage. Even at forty, Adele made a lovely picture as she stepped into the carriage, her curls bouncing about her face, under her cap. She wore a dress of lavender crape, whose shade had been chosen precisely for the salubrious effect upon her complexion, and, with a smile, Sara predicted that her mother would likely have almost as many admirers as Kitty that night.

This opinion was soon confirmed. Adele barely had time to greet their hostess before three male acquaintances appeared and bore her off to the card rooms. Sara could not feel this was entirely proper, as it left her and Kitty with Lady Haverstock. The lady, however, appeared undaunted as she said affectionately, "I am delighted to see both of you tonight. My son, I assure you, has been in despair, for fear something would keep you from attending!" She hesitated, then said, "I believe he intends to present you, Katherine, to his guardian, the Earl of Danver. I beg you will not let that gentleman overset you, my dear. He can appear quite fierce, but you must not regard it."

As Lady Haverstock spoke, Sara realized that Tom was approaching with a tall, dark-haired fellow who topped him by a full head; in short, with Danver. "Kitty!" Tom exclaimed as soon as he was close by. "Let me make my cousin Ned known to you. He's a bang-up fellow, and the seventh Earl of Danver.

Ned, this is Miss Katherine Farthingham. Oh, and her cousin, Miss Sara Farthingham."

Kitty curtsied, and gazed up at the Earl with a look calculated to speed any gentleman's pulse. As Tom looked on with pride, she murmured some sort of shy greeting. The Earl, however, merely regarded her coolly, through his glass, as he gave a slight bow and said, "Good evening, Miss Farthingham. I understand this is your first Season. I trust you are enjoying London?"

"Oh, yes! I never dreamt it would be so much fun!" Kitty answered, a trifle breathlessly. "Of course, I'd been to visit, before, but that was when I was still in the schoolroom, and so much was denied to me."

The Earl raised an eyebrow. "I wager that little is denied you now?"

Kitty blushed very prettily. "Oh, no. My Aunt Adele, and my cousin Sara, are so kind to me!"

"Ah, yes," the Earl said, raising his glass once more, "your cousin Sara. How do you do, Miss Farthingham?"

Sara met his eyes calmly. "Good evening, my lord," was all she said.

The Earl turned back to his ward. "I advise you, Tom, to waste no time claiming this dance with Miss Farthingham. Unless I am much mistaken, a number of her other beaux are come for that purpose."

Seeing that his guardian was correct, Tom hastily led Kitty to the dance floor. That left Sara alone with the Earl, and he said to her, "I should, of course, have ascertained that your cousin has received permission to waltz, but I could no longer bear watching my ward making calf eyes at her. Has she permission?"

"Yes," Sara replied rather stiffly.

"Have you?"

"*What?*" Instantly aware of her breach of manners, Sara said, more calmly, "Yes, my lord, I received permission, three years ago, in my first Season."

"Good. Then will you waltz with me?"

Good manners compelled Sara to say, "Yes, of course, my lord."

As they moved onto the floor, and the Earl put an arm around her waist, Danver laughed softly. "Come! Don't look as if you wish to eat me. Only consider the envy you are arousing in all these maternal breasts! You must know that although I am known to dance—purely from a sense of duty, I assure you—I am also known *never* to waltz. Too likely to arouse expectations I have no intention of fulfilling, you know," Danver confided.

"Then I wonder you are waltzing with me!" Sara retorted tartly.

Danver gazed down at her with a lazy smile. "Oh, but remember, we both know you detest me! Come, confess it, you've been planning a setdown for me."

Against her will, Sara laughed. "Well, to be frank, I had hoped to give you one." She paused, her eyes dancing. "I even envisioned that, perhaps, you might be late. And that, purely out of civility, Tom might have asked me to dance."

"And I should have entered upon this scene and thought you still Kitty?" the Earl suggested appreciatively. "Yes, and no doubt you hoped I should be so unwise as to say something to both of you, and then Tom should have set me in my place, right enough?" He laughed with her, before saying, "You have a *most* mischievous mind, Miss Farthingham, that is belied by your innocent appearance. Tell me, why have we never met before?"

Something closed over Sara, and her eyes ceased to dance, as she said, "We have, my lord."

"I don't mean yesterday!" he replied impatiently.

"Nor do I," said Sara evenly.

The Earl was silent for a moment before saying, "I see." His ready sense of humour caused him to chuckle at Sara's forbidding expression. "Now I have landed myself in the briars, haven't I? I collect that you mean to imply we've met several times, and that I should remember you? Well, I don't, and it's no use pretending otherwise. Though how I could forget so *original* a young lady is beyond me!"

In spite of herself, Sara laughed and her eyes met the Earl's. He smiled down at her. "That's better. Now, will you tell me when and where we've met?"

"Three years ago, my lord, at Almack's. You were used to choose young ladies—at random, I am persuaded—to dance. I was, occasionally, one of them. But it is not at all wonderful that you have forgotten. I was far too shy, that Season, to do more than nod to your questions and watch my feet," she answered shyly.

Danver stared down at Sara. "And these past two Seasons?"

Sara looked away as she answered. "My father died

shortly after my first Season, and I have had no taste
for parties, until Kitty came to town. Indeed, I
wished to put off my come-out, for my father was
very ill, even then, but he would not have it. I think
. . . I think he hoped to see me make a match, before he died. I'm afraid I failed him."

Presented only with the top of her head, Danver
answered Sara firmly. "He was quite right, you
know, to insist on your Season. Otherwise you must
have been twenty before your come-out. At least now
this is your second Season and you may be more at
ease." Sara smiled up at the Earl, grateful for his explanation, and he added, "I find it difficult to believe you failed your father, in any way."

"Oh, but I did," she said frankly. "He always
looked for me to be a beauty, as my mother was, and
you can scarcely say I succeeded at that! Nor could
he abide my turn for books or for the country."

"Puffing off your virtues at me?" Danver quizzed.

"You need not roast me, my lord," Sara said, unexpectedly grim. "I am well aware these are not considered assets in a young lady."

The easy mood between them was broken. Danver
was aware, suddenly, that he was, for reasons not altogether beyond his comprehension, considered a
Matrimonial Prize. He could not help wondering if
this was one more of those gambits, employed by a
female who had set her cap for him, and he answered, more coolly than he had intended, "I find
that I have little interest in, or comprehension of,
what constitutes the proper virtues for a young lady.

But I am sure there are any number of persons who could advise you."

Staring over her head, the Earl was startled to hear Sara say, in a murmur that was barely audible, "Did you know, I had forgotten how insufferably arrogant you can be?" Louder, she said coolly, "Of course. I had forgotten your poor opinion of my sex."

Danver was shaken. He had always prided himself on his easy manners and would have wagered that, while his male friends might know of his general contempt, no female should have cause to suspect it. And no woman had ever had the audacity to inform him that his conversation was less than pleasing. None of this passed through Edward's conscious mind. He only found himself goaded into saying, "There you are out, Miss Farthingham. I do not detest your entire sex. There are certain members of it who are honest enough to name themselves for what they are!"

Sara's eyes were blazing, as she met his, but her voice was ice. "I collect you mean the muslin set. I understand you perfectly, my lord."

She might have said more, but Danver cut her off ruthlessly, saying, "Well, you should not! And if you do, you should certainly not admit it."

Mischief won out over anger, and Sara replied demurely, "But, my lord, you should not have mentioned the subject, if you did not wish me to speak of it."

Danver met her eyes, ruefully. "Particularly as

you had already warned me that you were an unconventional young lady?"

Together, they laughed, and the last strains of the waltz found them still in accord. At the edge of the dance floor, Danver relinquished Sara, saying so softly that only she could hear, "I'd best go find some chit to dance with. Otherwise, Lord knows what the gossips will say about us!"

The gossips, in fact, were at a loss. That the Earl of Danver had asked Sara to waltz was indeed an unprecedented occurrence, but the notion of considering quiet Miss Sara Farthingham a serious source of interest, for the Earl, seemed absurd. For the moment, it seemed more amusing to watch a certain young Duke and the daughter of a certain elderly Baron, and lay odds as to how soon he was likely to come up to scratch!

Sara was oblivious of all this, content to watch the dancers as they followed the music of an exceptionally fine orchestra. Flowers and candles were everywhere, and Sara had just turned to admire the arrangement beside her, when she heard a familiar voice exclaim, "Sara!"

"Charles! Whatever are you doing here? We thought you on the Continent. In Vienna, at last word."

He grinned at her, Major Charles Farthingham, Kitty's brother. Taking Sara's hand, he teased, "What sort of welcome is that? I'm home on leave. Just got into London tonight. Walthers told me I'd find you and Kitty and my Aunt Adele here, so I came. Not precisely dressed for it, but I knew no lady would turn away a soldier in uniform," he confided.

Sara could not help but agree. Nor could she help being aware of the envious glances she drew from the other young ladies present. Unconsciously, she tilted her chin upward and smiled wider as she said, "I *do* welcome you, Charles. But tell me, what did Kitty say when she saw you?".

He laughed. "She didn't! I couldn't get near her. Lord, when I left England, she was fourteen and I thought her impossible! Now I find she's become a beauty. So I decided to come and talk with you, instead. May I?"

There was no reserve in her smile, as Sara nodded to Charles. She had always had a *tendre* for this fair-haired cousin of hers, who might well be said to rival Kitty in looks. He wasn't overly tall, but his form was of the sort most men might envy, and his head was capped with curls. As they moved to nearby chairs, Sara recollected, with a smile, that many young ladies had been known to find his green-grey eyes irresistible. Well, tonight Sara had no desire to resist her joy at seeing Charles again. And what harm? He was her cousin. "You've changed," she said quietly.

He looked at Sara and nodded. "I have, and so have you." Charles paused, studying her, then added, "The changes suit you. I heard about your father, Sara, and I'm sorry. It must have been a difficult time for you. How do you go on, now?"

She made an effort to keep her smile. "Well enough, especially with Kitty here to keep us gay.

Indeed, I can hardly tell you how pleased my mother is to have such a beauty to launch!"

Charles frowned at her words. "And you? You've found no one?" She shook her head, not meeting his eyes. "Not even a *tendre* for anyone?" Charles persisted.

Sara tossed her head and laughed then. "Oh, as for *tendres!* Well I've always had those, as *you* should know."

Charles chuckled. "So I should! I've not forgotten how you sent me off, with a flower and a kiss, when I left to join my regiment."

Sara grinned wryly. "Nor have I forgotten how little you appreciated my gifts!"

For a moment, they were silent, with the ease of old friends. Then Sara asked quietly, "And you? Have you found anyone?"

A brief shadow rested on Charles's face. Then firmly he said, "I have. Her name is Lisette, and I plan to marry her, no matter what my father has to say."

"Tell me about her," Sara said softly.

The frown disappeared, and Charles looked at his cousin, without seeing her, his thoughts very far away. Lord Danver, watching them from a vantage point some distance away, saw only that Miss Farthingham and her companion appeared to be on quite intimate terms. A decision, half-formed, to leave early, was banished without conscious effort. His conclusions would have been drastically altered, had he been close enough to hear Charles say, "She's the most lovely, delicate girl I've ever seen. A lot like my sister, Kitty, except that Lisette is dark-haired, and no one could ever call her spoilt. A man only has to meet Lisette to want to take care of her."

"You mentioned your father," Sara said hesitantly. "Have you told him, then?"

Charles frowned again. "I hinted at it, in a letter home, months ago. My mother wrote that my father won't have me marrying a foreigner, and that they have plans for me, at home."

Sara was sympathetic. "But it doesn't signify, does it? He can't forbid the banns, can he?"

Charles shook his head, and forced a smile. "No. But it would be pleasanter if my bride were assured of a warm welcome."

"Well, she shall always have one from me!" Sara promised.

Impulsively, oblivious of the eyes that watched, Charles pressed his cousin's hand as he said, "I knew I could count on you, Sara! You'll love Lisette, I know you will."

They both started to stand, when a slight figure launched herself into the Major's arms, crying, "Charlie! Charlie! Why didn't you tell me you were back?"

"Kitty! Because I've just come to town, silly puss! Pleased to see me?"

Sara moved away, to leave them alone, and immediately encountered Tom Haverstock, who stood nearby watching. "Her brother," she explained, before he could speak.

Tom grinned. "I know. How I wish she'd greet me

that way, just once!" Then, teasingly, he said, "Kitty tells me you have a *tendre* for him, as well?"

Sara dimpled, entering into the spirit of things. "Of course! I think everyone must."

From behind them a dry voice said, "At least among the ladies!"

Sara turned, looking up at the Earl, who added, "You seem very close to your, er, cousin, Miss Farthingham. Is there, perhaps, an understanding?"

"Surely that's a rather impertinent question, my lord?" Sara replied coolly.

Tom laughed. "Wants to be sure he's safe in your company, Sara! Ned can't abide females who may be setting their caps at him."

Conscious of a lump in her throat, Sara heard Danver, through a haze, as he spoke sharply to Tom. "You've had too much to drink, Tom, and I wish you will go away!"

By the time Haverstock had complied, Sara had herself in hand again, and she was able to say, "I do not choose to discuss the matter with you, my lord."

Hearing the catch, in her voice, Danver reached his own conclusions. Grimly he said, "It's that way, is it. You've a *tendre* for him, and he has none for you?"

Swiftly Sara met his eyes. "No, you don't understand! Indeed, Charles is always very kind to me."

The corner of Danver's mouth twitched as he said, "Kind? Indeed. But it's not kindness you want, if you've a *tendre* for someone!"

Sara's eyes fell; she did not deny it. It was *not* kindness she wanted, from the man she had a *tendre*

for. As she stared at the floor, she heard the Earl say
roughly, "He's not worth it, you know." Then,
smoothly, at the sound of people approaching, "Will
you allow me to take you in to supper, Miss Farthingham? I wish to hear more about your sketches."

Sara was hard pressed to conceal a gurgle of laughter as she replied demurely, "Why, thank you, my
Lord Danver."

She placed a hand on his arm, and they moved
toward the supper room, as a matron audibly sniffed,
directly behind them. Sara felt dizzy, her sense of
humour warring with common sense. She ought not
to be going in to supper with this man, and she
ought to correct his misapprehensions. A chuckle escaped her. Immediately Danver's eyes were on her,
questioning. The chuckle became a ripple of laughter as she said, "*Sketches* indeed! I fear I am ruining
your reputation, Lord Danver."

His mouth twisted into a grin. "Do you mean to
tell me you *don't* sketch, Miss Farthingham?"

Her eyes dancing, Sara said, "That is precisely
what I mean to tell you! I've no turn for it at all.
The difficulty is that Mrs. Watson knows it."

Danver frowned. "That gorgon who overheard us,
you mean?" At Sara's confirming nod, he tilted back
his head and laughed. "I think you may be right,
Miss Farthingham, in saying that you're in a fair way
to ruining my reputation. What do you propose to
do about it? Blacken it further?"

"What a tempting notion!" Sara retorted, without
thinking.

The Earl barely heard her. He was staring across

the room to where Tom, Kitty, and Charles were already seated at a table. "Shall we join them?" he asked Sara, pointing out the party.

She looked up at him uncertainly. "I should like to, but we need not, if you would prefer to sit elsewhere."

At the sight of her anxious upturned face, Danver frowned and said, a trifle impatiently, "By all means, let us join them."

Tom spotted them first. "Ned! Sara! Come join us."

"That was our intention," Edward replied dryly. "Hello, again, Miss Farthingham. Sir?"

Hastily Tom performed the introduction. "This is Major Charles Farthingham, Kitty's brother. Charles, this is my cousin Edward, seventh Earl of Danver."

The gentlemen exchanged greetings, and for a few minutes the talk was of military matters. Then Danver left to procure plates of food for Sara and himself. Charles immediately turned to Sara, who was seated beside him, and said, "An earl, eh? Doing very well for yourself. Plan to bring him up to scratch?"

The question was asked in a teasing undertone, but Sara answered seriously, "I doubt very much that it would be possible."

Charles's expression softened. "So that's how it is, is it? Shall I call him out for you?"

Again, the tone was gently teasing, and Sara tried to match it. "I hardly see how that would aid me, Charles."

"Shall I contrive to make him jealous?" the Major persisted.

Seeing that her cousin was only half in jest, Sara felt herself at a loss, and bowed her head in confusion. It was at that moment that the Earl returned, having filled the plates hastily, with little regard for what he took. Sara's distress was not lost on him, nor the fact that Charles's eyes were on her. His expression grim, Danver set one of the plates in front of Sara. She looked up at him quickly, even managing a smile as she said, "Thank you, my lord."

Danver's expression softened as he seated himself on her other side. Meanwhile, Tom was saying, "Ned, it's the most famous thing: Major Farthingham fought in the Peninsula!"

Danver nodded. "I had guessed as much. Do you rejoin your regiment soon, Major?"

Charles shook his head. "Of late, I've been a courier rather than a fighting man, and at the moment am on indefinite leave."

The significance of this was not lost on Danver, and he asked swiftly, "You think us finally at peace, then?"

Charles hesitated before replying, "For the time."

"But surely Napoleon is beaten?" Sara protested.

Charles made an effort to smile at her. "To be sure. But I have learned not to underestimate the man. Never mind, I'm overly cautious. Tell me, instead, the latest gossip."

Tom and Kitty readily obliged. The Earl and Sara remained quiet, content to listen. A short time later, the party returned to the ballroom, where Lord

Danver made his excuses and withdrew. Sara watched his departing back, well aware of the stares he attracted. She was less aware of the ones she drew. The attention of a man such as the Earl of Danver could not but help a young lady's social advancement, and Sara found her hand solicited for every dance that remained.

When Adele Farthingham finally gathered her charges to return home, she found both damsels worn to a thread with dancing. It was a circumstance which could not but gratify the lady. Nor was she displeased to discover that Charles was back in England. "Charlie, dear boy!" she cried when she saw him. "Where are you staying?"

"With friends in Stratton Street," he informed her cheerfully, "though I expect to haunt *your* house this next week or so."

Adele Farthingham dimpled with pleasure, until she remembered, "Your parents, Charles. Have you seen them yet?" At his negative shake of the head, she said, "But surely you plan to post down there, right away?"

He gave her an odd smile. "No, I've some business to attend to in London first. I'll post down later."

Satisfied with this reply, and having extracted a promise from him to call the next morning, Adele swept Sara and Kitty out to the waiting coach.

4

It was not to be expected that Charles would escape unscathed from an encounter with his Aunt Adele. Nor did he. She extracted from him a promise to escort his sister and his cousin to several forthcoming affairs. "For it is not as if you have any other young lady to escort. Or do you?" Adele asked frankly.

"Not here in London," Charles replied promptly, a twinkle in his eye.

"Good. Then there cannot be the least objection," the redoutable woman said, with satisfaction.

There was not, at any rate, any major objection, and Major Farthingham agreed. It did not occur to Adele that certain gossips might draw conclusions from Charles's frequent escort of his cousin Sara. It did occur to Charles. However, when he spoke of it, hesitantly, to Sara, and asked if she minded, Sara retorted, "Nonsense! You must know that, for such an ape-leader as myself, such gossip can only enhance my standing!"

Sara spoke in jest, but Adele Farthingham was quick to note, in the days that followed, that Sara had indeed begun (finally!) to acquire a circle of admirers. She did not, however, ascribe this to Charles's presence so much as to the kind condescension of the seventh Earl of Danver in asking Sara to stand up for two dances with him, whenever they chanced to be at the same ball. It was very gratifying. Particularly as Sara was a girl of much common sense, and hardly likely to commit the folly of bestowing her heart on a hardened bachelor.

Lord Danver was aware that his mild interest in Miss Sara Farthingham was causing a stir, and dismissed it. He would have been exceedingly angry, had he known the full extent of the gossip being relayed to his mother at Swinford Abbey, but he was not aware of it and, therefore, was feeling quite in charity with the world a few weeks later as he tooled his high-perch phaeton through the park. It was pulled by two matching greys, and was the envy of many young aspirants to fashion, who lacked his skill with the reins. Danver had just swept past two antiquated barouches, when he spied a familiar figure walking along. At once he pulled up his horses. "Miss Farthingham! Good day."

Immediately, her head jerked up, and Sara looked at the Earl, with dismay and confusion evident on her face. With effort, she managed to say, "Good day, my lord."

Sara waited a moment before approaching the phaeton, as though expecting Danver to drive on. He did not, but continued to stare at her with his piercing eyes. As she stood, her anxious face turned up to his, Sara heard Danver say, "Would you care for a drive about the park, Miss Farthingham?"

Hesitantly Sara said, "Thank you, I should."

Immediately, Danver's well trained tiger dismounted and assisted Sara into the phaeton. Danver nodded at him. "I shall see you back at the house, Timothy."

"Right, guv'nor."

If Sara was surprised at this order, she did not say so. As the horses moved forward, the Earl glanced at Sara and said, in his usual abrupt way, "Something is wrong, Miss Farthingham. Will you tell me what it is?"

"Why . . . why do you say that?" Sara asked, startled.

Danver sighed, a trifle impatiently. "Miss Farthingham, I cut my eyeteeth years ago. You are walking, alone, in the park, without your maid. I cannot believe you are so rash, or so careless of your reputation, as to do so without cause. Therefore, something is either amiss, or you have come out for an assignation. I think, indeed I hope, you have too much pride to come out here to meet a fellow who professes to care for you, yet would ask you to behave so improperly. And when I saw you, you were looking much distressed."

Sara looked at him wryly. "And I thought that, at this hour, I should meet no one I knew, and it would not matter."

"Well, you were out!" Danver retorted, then added, more gently, "Please believe, Miss Farthingham, that I should like to be of assistance, if I could."

Sara was silent. She had danced with Lord Danver many times since Lady Haverstock's ball and, inevitably, they had conversed. But it had been the sort of light banter suitable to two members of the *ton* enjoying a mild flirtation. Danver had never given Sara reason to believe, until now, that he possessed this serious, concerned side. It was not at all surprising, therefore, that Sara should have felt at a loss. Indeed, the majority of London's *haut ton* would have been surprised to hear that Lord Danver was capable of concern for anyone save himself. Only his tenants, servants, and close friends had ever seen this side of him. Yet, when his concern had been aroused, no one was more amiable or more helpful than the seventh Earl of Danver. Or more discreet. It was this last quality which led to the general opinion that Danver was a hardhearted creature.

Propriety spoke against confiding in Lord Danver. So did common sense, yet Sara found herself doing so. "Very well. This morning, when I rang for my maid, whom I share with Kitty, she was late answering my bell. When she did arrive, she told me that she had been helping Kitty dress. You must understand that this is most unusual, that my cousin rarely rises before nine or ten o'clock. I was concerned that something was amiss, and I went in to see her. But she was gone out, alone. I . . . I had no reason to believe that perhaps . . . perhaps Kitty had arranged an assignation, and I assumed it must be here, in the park. Where else could she hope to meet a man, unnoticed? I came after her, hoping to find her before anyone saw or recognized her. But I've had no success."

Danver listened to this explanation with creditable patience, then demanded, "Did you never think of your own reputation?"

Sara shook her head impatiently. "I am no green miss, my lord. What would be fatal to a girl in her first Season, I might well contrive to carry off. As I told you, I did not expect to encounter anyone I knew. No one could see Kitty and not stare, but I might well pass unnoticed. And, in any case, Kitty has been placed in my mother's care, and *someone* must look after her."

"To be sure," Danver said tersely, "but why must it be you?"

Hearing the anger in his voice, Sara said earnestly, "You must not be thinking me a martyr, Lord Danver! I assure you that, in general, Kitty is a most pleasant companion for me and I am enjoying her visit."

"Oh, yes, I quite see you and Kitty have so much in common," Danver said sarcastically. "Doing it much too brown, Miss Farthingham. Next you will tell me your cousin is a bluestocking!"

Sara laughed. "Well, no, we do not have so very much in common. But Kitty is an amiable girl, if a trifle volatile. And I do enjoy her visit, for you must know how much happier my mother is since she arrived. She, my mother, has always been disappointed I was not a beauty," Sara explained frankly, "and she cannot but enjoy taking Kitty about."

"If she prefers your cousin to you, she is a fool," Danver retorted, equally frankly. Sara looked at him, astonished, but before she could collect her wits, Danver shattered the compliment by adding, "I never could abide brainless chits, but then, I am informed that I am sadly lacking in taste. Nevertheless, I don't think *you* lack for sense, Miss Farthingham."

Her voice a trifle unsteady, Sara managed to say, "Nor do I, my lord." Then, primly, "But you are forgetting, you offered your assistance, and we must look for Kitty."

"No, we must not!" Danver replied unequivocally. "By now, she will surely have returned home and, in any case, we would scarcely have room to take her up with us."

"But I would get down!" Sara protested.

"Another excellent reason not to search for your cousin Kitty," he retorted. "No, I think I shall drive you home, instead."

Sara was about to protest hotly, when a horse drew abreast of the phaeton, and a familiar voice exclaimed, "Sara! What the deuce are you doing here?"

"Major?" The Earl's voice was cold and haughty.

"Oh! Beg pardon, Danver. No offense intended. Just a bit of a shock, seeing my cousin out so early. No need to worry, of course, if she's in your company," Charles added hastily.

"I'm happy you realize that," Danver said, surveying Charles sardonically. "Do you find it so amazing that Miss Farthingham might choose to drive out with me?"

Sara, aware of the equivocal nature of her situation, blushed, and quickly intervened. "Good morning, Charles. Is that your horse? He seems a beauty."

Major Charles Farthingham nodded gratefully at his cousin. "So he is." He hesitated, then, with a wary glance at Lord Danver, said, "If I call, in an hour or so, Sara, will I find you home?"

"If you are asking how long we shall be," Danver interrupted, "I was about to drive Miss Farthingham home, now. Whether she will receive you is another matter."

"Of course I will!" Sara retorted indignantly. "Indeed," she went on, more softly, "I shall be quite pleased to see you, Charles."

"Good!" He smiled warmly at her. "I shall see you then. Good day, Lord Danver."

"Good day, Major."

As Charles turned his horse to ride away, Danver let his horses shoot forward. As soon as they were out of earshot of her cousin, Sara demanded, "Must you be so rude to Charles?"

Danver glanced at her and asked, curious, "Are you really angry because I was rude to him, or because I told him you had chosen to come out driving with me? Is he to believe you spend all your days alone, thinking of him? It will not do, Miss Farthingham." Sara started to protest, but Danver gave her no chance. "Come, Miss Farthingham, I grant you this cannot be pleasant for you, but you must realize that running away from the truth won't resolve anything. I should advise you to let your cousin see you, often, in the company of other men!"

Forced to turn his attention to the matter of threading his horses through the busy London streets, Danver did not see the wry expression with which Sara regarded him. After several minutes, she said softly, "No doubt you would know, my lord."

"In this case, I would!" he confirmed.

Apparently feeling that he had said enough, Lord Danver was content to travel the rest of the way in silence. When they reached the house in Park Street, Sara said, "Will you come up, my lord?"

Danver shook his head. "No, I've business to attend to." Then, helping her down from the phaeton while a nearby link boy stood at the horses' heads, he added, "I do believe you will find your cousin safely at home, Miss Farthingham."

Sara gave him a doubtful smile, then mounted the steps. It was immediately plain to her that her absence had not gone unnoticed. Walthers hinted as much, as he admitted her, and Sara found both her mother and Kitty waiting in the Yellow Saloon. Adele greeted Sara sternly, saying, "Sara Farthingham, where have you been? Betsy informs me you went out Alone! I cannot credit it. You! So Lost to Propriety! Have you no sense whatsoever?"

Kitty sat beside her aunt, the picture of innocence. Removing her chip hat, Sara answered, as calmly as she was able, "I was not out alone, Mama. Lord Danver took me for a drive about the park."

"Lord Danver?" Kitty demanded. "He took you for a drive? In his phaeton? Tom says—"

"That will be enough, Katherine!" Adele cut short her niece. Then, thoughtfully, she said to Sara, "Danver? To be sure, an earl would be quite a feather in your cap, my dear. However, Lord Danver is a special case. Everyone has quite made up their mind that he will never marry. Still, he can only add to your credit, so long as he does not become too particular in his attentions, and so long as you do not develop a *tendre* for him."

"Yes, Mama," was Sara's dutiful reply. Quickly, to turn the subject, she said, "We saw Charles. He intends to call this morning."

"What? How marvelous! I was to drive out, with Peter Cheshire, but it don't signify. Peter can come in and sit, instead," was Kitty's delighted reply.

Adele also was pleased. "How delightful. I must see Cook and tell her to send up something special for lunch, in case Charlie will stay for it."

As her mother left to carry out this resolution, Sara sank onto a window seat. Immediately, Kitty joined her, full of eager questions. "Were you really with Lord Danver? Tom says he *never* takes any woman up in his phaeton. Did he let you handle the reins? Has he a *tendre* for you? When did you arrange to drive out with him?"

Sara hesitated. She wanted very much to speak frankly with Kitty, and find out the truth about her cousin's disappearance. It seemed impossible that Kitty could talk so carelessly if she had indeed slipped out that morning for an assignation. And if she had not, Sara had no desire to set such notions in her cousin's head. Furthermore, blunt accusations could only lead to denial and an estrangement between Sara and her cousin. On the other hand, Sara found she had no taste for lies. In the end, she compromised with part of the truth. "You must not be imagining anything so romantic," Sara said wryly. "Indeed, so far from making love to me, his lordship read me a scold. And nothing, I am persuaded, would ever convince him to allow me to handle his cattle."

Disappointed, Kitty pouted. "Well, I can not understand why you do not make the least push to fix your interest with Lord Danver. Have you no ambition whatsoever?"

Sara laughed. "I fear not. Much good it would do me, anyway! But tell me, Kitty, how did you spend the morning?" she could not resist asking.

Kitty flushed and looked away. "Oh, I did nothing that would interest you. You must excuse me, for I must change my dress if Charlie is coming to call. I hope we shall be able to have a cozy chat with him."

Kitty's hopes were destined to disappointment. By the time Major Charles Farthingham arrived, the

Yellow Saloon was already filled with Kitty's admirers, who demanded her attention. The most favored of these was, of course, Peter Cheshire, since she had been pledged to drive out with him. All of the young men were on excellent terms with Sara, who tended to treat them as the younger brothers she had never had. Thus, several of them felt free to quiz her over her conquest of Lord Scantham, an elderly fellow who had begun to make Sara the object of his rather outmoded gallantry. She took it in good part, but was rather relieved when Charles's entrance effectively put an end to this banter. He greeted Kitty and his aunt, then contrived to draw Sara aside, so that he might talk with her. "Good morning again, cousin," he said lightly.

"Good morning, Charles," she returned warmly. "You seem in excellent spirits."

He laughed softly. "I should be. I've had news from Lisette. Her parents have consented to the match!"

Startled, Sara said, "But I thought . . . Do you mean to say they *hadn't* consented, before?"

Charles looked a bit sheepish as he bent his fair head closer to hers. "Not really, though I was certain they would, once they became accustomed to the idea. But Lisette is so young that, of course, they hesitated."

"How young?" Sara asked hesitantly.

"Seventeen. She's not yet out, really, so no announcement will be made for a few months," Charles replied.

Sara tried to picture her cousin with a schoolroom miss. As though reading her thoughts and doubts, Charles went on, "I know how it must seem, Sara, but she's older than you might expect, for her years. Lisette's family was forced to flee France, when she was still a mere baby. Fortunately, her mother's relatives, in Vienna, could take them in, but war has been a part of her life for as long as she can remember."

Sara nodded, then asked, "And your parents? When will you speak to them about Lisette?"

He smiled ruefully. "I must seem a coward, Sara, staying in London, when I might post home. But I know they would only send me back, saying I should look at the Season's young ladies. This way, I shall say that I have and that I still prefer my Lisette."

Sara was thoughtful for several moments. Finally she said, "I must say, if it were I, I should consign my parents to the devil, and marry Lisette out of hand. Then, if they continued to object, I should tell them that they must accept Lisette, or not see me again."

Charles was appalled. "Pretty behaviour that would be! And who would present Lisette, or take her about, if my family snubbed her? She's not so resolute as you, Sara. Lisette needs kindness. No, I'll wait. My parents must come about, soon."

Sara only had time to give Charles's hand a quick squeeze, in sympathy, before her mother claimed him, with a mock scold. "Charlie Farthingham! Have you no time at all for your old Aunt Adele?"

He turned to her with a smile. "*Old* Aunt Adele?

Humbug! You know very well you look young enough to be having a Season yourself!"

As Charles devoted himself to Sara's mother, good manners compelled Sara to join in the circle that surrounded Kitty.

5

For several days, Kitty gave Sara no further cause for concern. Gradually Sara relaxed and decided that the flirtation (if, indeed, Kitty had slipped out that morning for an assignation) was at an end. The usual round of parties, breakfasts, drives in the park, and evenings at Almack's continued, and Kitty seemed to favour none of her suitors over the others. The seventh Earl of Danver continued to appear, frequently, at the same functions as the Farthingham ladies, and he once, jestingly, told Sara, "You must know that it is my duty to study *my* cousin's interest in *your* cousin."

If, however, he spent more time at Sara's side than at Kitty's, she was not about to protest.

It was in this mood of complacence that Sara dressed for an evening at Almack's. Descending the stairs, Sara and her mother found Kitty waiting, and looking despondent. Kitty was dressed in a fetching creation, of pale pink satin and lace, eminently suitable for Almack's, but her voice was weary as she said, "Aunt Adele, please don't be angry, with me, but I have the headache and feel too ill for dancing."

Sara was inclined to suspicion, but her cousin did, indeed, look very pale. Adele was all concern. "Poor child! Of course you need not go. We, none of us, shall go to Almack's."

"Oh, no!" Kitty's eyes were wide with dismay. "You must not stay home, on my account. Charles is sure to be there. And . . . and Lord Danver and . . . and Sir Carstairs. Surely, Sara can not wish to stay home?"

Touched, Sara said, "I own, I should like to go."

Adele hugged Kitty and promised, "We'll be home early."

With a sweet, sad smile, Kitty insisted, "You need not, you know. I shall go straight up to bed, and be asleep before you even reach Almack's. You need not, I assure you, shorten your pleasure, on my account."

In the end, Adele and Sara left, a trifle reluctantly, with Sara guiltily trying to banish the suspicion she still felt. Feeling the need for something to divert her thoughts, Sara was pleased to find that, although they arrived early, Charles was already at Almack's. With a quick, courteous greeting for Sara and her mother, he asked impatiently after his sister.

"She has the headache, poor thing," Adele explained, "and was obliged to remain at home. She is such a good girl, Charles, that you would not credit it!"

One glance at Charles's face sufficed to inform Sara that, indeed, he did not credit it. After a few minutes of chatter, Adele was drawn off, to the card room, by one of her admirers. As soon as she was out of earshot, Sara turned to her cousin. "What is it you fear, Charles?" she demanded, adding dryly, "Come, come. I must already suspect the worst of Kitty, you know."

Charles nodded curtly. "Very well. A week ago, Kitty asked me if I would take her to a masquerade. I told her that I would not, that it would be most improper for her to attend one. She was not precisely complacent and, tonight, at the Pantheon—"

Sara interrupted Charles, gripping his arm tightly. "Charles! Yesterday, I saw her with a domino!"

Charles swore under his breath, then demanded, "And you thought to tell no one? You were not, in the least, alarmed?"

Dismayed, Sara replied, "I wasn't sure what I had seen. Kitty whisked it out of sight, at once. But when you mentioned the masquerade, it came to me that it must have been a domino."

"What colour?" Charles demanded.

"Green," was the prompt reply.

"Well, at least it shall be easy to see." Charles sighed.

"What do you mean to do?" Sara asked.

"Go to the Pantheon, and try to keep my heedless sister from ruining herself," Charles answered grimly. "Though I've half a mind to let her be. It would serve her well if she had to return home in disgrace!"

"So it might," Sara agreed, "but recollect that Kitty is in my mother's care, and it is she, not Kitty, who will be most blamed."

Charles nodded. "I know, and it is one more reason for me to be angry at her!"

Sara was thoughtful for a brief moment, then said urgently, "If we leave at once, we may still catch her at home."

"*We?*" Shock echoed through Charles's voice. "No, my girl, you'll stay here! I've no thought to trade your reputation for Kitty's. If I go alone, and find my sister, we may contrive to bring her off unscathed. But I can conceive of no way to leave, with you, that would not cause the tattle boxes to bandy your name about."

"As if I cared for that!" Sara said uncertainly.

"Well, I do!" Charles retorted roughly. "And so must you, if you are honest. It is only that you conceive it your duty to rescue my sister, and I tell you, frankly, that I can contrive it well enough without you."

Sara drew her brows together, acknowledging the wisdom of what Charles said. Still, she added, "But, Charles, you cannot go to our house and ask for Kitty."

"I do not mean to," he answered bluntly, "for I place no dependence on her being there. No, I go straightaway to the Pantheon. Indeed, I must, if I am to return with Kitty before eleven."

"You'll bring her here?" Sara asked in surprise.

"It will silence any tongues that might claim to have seen her at the masquerade, if she is known to have been at Almack's tonight," Charles explained. "But if I cannot return in time, I must take her home and hope for the best. And now, I can linger no longer. Let us trust fortune favours me!"

Sara let him go, as aware as Charles of the need for haste. Then, knowing that her tête-à-tête with Charles could not have gone unnoticed, Sara forced a smile to her face, and turned to watch the dancing. It was only a few moments before Lord Scantham was at her side. That Sara could greet Lord Scantham with relief and even something approaching pleasure was a measure of the anxiety Sara felt. Lord Scantham was both surprised and gratified at his unusually warm reception. "Ah, Miss Farthingham, you are always in such spirits that it quite exalts my own!" Gallantly bowing from the waist, his face flushing from the exercise, he went on, "May I dare hope you will honour me with a dance?"

Lord Scantham had never before had the temerity to venture such a question to Sara, feeling that his corpulence could only render such a thing absurd. The words were scarce out before he regretted them, but to his delighted surprise, Sara accepted. To be sure, it was only a country dance and one was afforded, therefore, little opportunity for conversation; nevertheless, his lordship was flattered, certain that his suit was prospering nicely.

Sara, though she could not enjoy the notion of being partnered with such a figure of fun, felt it preferable to being quizzed by the various matrons

who had been bearing down on her when Lord Scantham appeared. She had no desire to answer questions concerning her cousin. Either cousin.

Had his notions of propriety not been so nice,
Lord Scantham must have pressed Sara to dance
with him again, immediately following the country
dance, so emboldened was he by Sara's reception of
him. Propriety prevailed, however, and he gracefully
retired, promising to fetch her a glass of lemonade.

Her next partner, who had had Miss Sara Farthingham described to him as a young woman of much
common sense, was moved to tell his friends later
that it was no such thing! That Miss Sara was as scat-
ter-minded as her young cousin. For this impression,
Charles and Kitty were responsible. Though Sara
knew they could not possibly have had time to return, Sara could not keep from watching the door.
She was very surprised, therefore, to find Lord Danver waiting for her at the end of the next dance, for
she had not seen him enter. If she was surprised, she
was also relieved, knowing that, with this partner, at
least, she need not stand on ceremony. "Good evening, my lord," she said with an easy smile.

Danver looked down at her with his piercing eyes,
and said with concern, "I should ask you to dance,
Miss Farthingham, but I am persuaded you are a
trifle fatigued, and would prefer to sit."

"Well, I own I should," Sara admitted frankly,
"though I've no wish to appear, in your eyes, one of
those vapourish, poor-spirited creatures who are always tired!"

"Impossible!" Danver assured Sara as he guided

her to a chair. Then, gently fanning her with the elegant fan he extracted from her grasp, he went on, in a quizzing tone, "Indeed, you must know, Miss Farthingham, that I find you the most intrepid female of my acquaintance!"

Sara laughed. "How unhandsome of you! I collect you mean to say you find me a burly, coming female! I wonder you even care to be seen with me?"

Danver grinned, showing his teeth. "Ah, but you forget. You blackened my reputation the first time we were introduced, and thus I've none left for you to destroy."

"I collect you mean our *second* meeting!" Sara corrected him swiftly.

"*I* would hardly call the first a *meeting*, more like a pitched battle, I should have said!" Danver countered. "And recollect that I had no notion I was addressing Miss Sara Farthingham, not her cousin Katherine."

"Had you known, you would not have addressed me at all, would you?" Sara said, with a smile.

"I would not," Danver agreed cordially, adding, "I can only be grateful for the mistake."

Fighting an unaccustomed shyness, Sara struggled to find a light reply. "Ah, I collect, from what Tom tells me, that you enjoy *sporting your canvas?*"

Danver gave a short laugh, then shook his head at her. "Unkind, Miss Farthingham!"

He might have added more, but at the sound of an altercation there, Sara's eyes flew to the door. It was only some provincial, trying to enter Almack's wearing pantaloons instead of the obligatory knee breeches, and he was given short shrift by the patronesses. Assured that the matter had nothing to do with her cousins, Sara turned back to Lord Danver. He was watching her, his eyes narrowed, with interest. "Who are you watching for?" he asked abruptly.

With anyone else, Sara might have dissembled, but as it was Lord Danver, she said honestly, "My cousin."

To her astonishment, Sara heard her fan snap. Startled, she looked up at the Earl and found his eyes blazing with anger. His voice, however, was cool as he said, "Indeed? May I suggest a little more pride, Miss Farthingham? I've no doubt the Major is quite skilled at paying his addresses to young ladies, but surely you have not mistaken a mere flirtation for something more serious?" Seeing her dismay, he went on thoughtfully, "Perhaps you've not had much experience, Miss Farthingham, but I tell you that I have seen you and your cousin together and I cannot believe there is anything more than respect, on his side."

"I am well aware of Charles's feelings," Sara replied stiffly.

Puzzled, Danver said, "Do you hope, then, to change his mind? To somehow attach him to you? I tell you, you are going about it the wrong way, if you are always watching the door for him."

The temptation to explain his error was powerful, but Sara resisted it. Rising to her feet, she said coolly, with an assurance she was far from feeling, "You must excuse me, my lord. I see one of my particular friends, wishing to speak with me."

Again there was the sound of snapping, and Sara's fan, when Danver returned it, was broken in several places. Danver, however, offered no apologies, merely bowing before he strode away. Sharp eyes, though not Sara's, noted that he chose to dance every dance, though none with Miss Sara Farthingham.

Charles, upon leaving Almack's, had no trouble hiring a hack. His first destination was Stratton Street to borrow a domino, then on to the Pantheon. In spite of the delay, which fretted Charles, they arrived in good time. Charles arranged his mask, then descended from the hack and gave orders to the driver, before disappearing inside. The driver of the hack, muttering to himself about the odd humours of *swells*, resigned himself to an annoying, but profitable, wait.

The Pantheon, though magnificent, brought no pleasure to Charles's eyes; he found it both vulgar and pretentious. He looked, first, for Kitty in the main ballroom, wandering past the boxes and alcoves. Kitty was nowhere to be seen, and his mood was not improved by the attempt of a very persistent female to accompany him. Indeed, Charles could only curse his sister's want of sense, in coming, and the intentions of the blackguard who had brought her. It was in this mood that Charles decided to search among the saloons for his sister. As he was about to enter the first, a slim figure hurtled toward him. A green domino, blond curls, and a frightened, maskless face were recognized, and Charles caught the figure as she was about to brush past him. "Let me go!" the girl cried breathlessly, beating her fists against his chest.

"Quiet!" he commanded into her ear. "It's Charles."

"Charlie!" she sobbed thankfully.

Frowning, he began to ask, "What is it, Kitten? What . . . ?"

The answer came striding toward them, a tall figure in a black domino. It was obvious, from the astonished look he gave Charles, and his snarl, that he had been pursuing Kitty. Abruptly he halted and gave a short bark of laughter. "Found someone more to your taste, have you? Watch out for her, my friend, she's a tease!"

"I wasn't teasing!" Kitty sobbed against Charles's chest.

Charles squeezed Kitty warningly, but the fellow turned on his heel and strode away before Charles could say a word. Charles would have followed, but for Kitty. It was of utmost importance that he get her out of there and into the waiting hack. Nevertheless, he could not resist demanding, "Is that the fellow who brought you?"

Kitty was still sobbing. "No! And you were right, I should not have come. When we arrived, I saw at once that it would not do, and I said I wanted to go home. He refused and I told him how horrid he was and I said I would go home alone and he said no and I ran away and then that man pulled off my mask and tried to kiss me and I ran away from *him* and then you came along and . . . Oh, Charles, I'm so glad you came!"

As he listened to his sister, Charles's expression had grown steadily more grim. He was not without sympathy for Kitty, but when he spoke, his voice was curt. "Yes, well, put your mask back on. Yes, I know it's been ripped, and you shall have to hold it in place, but you need only do so until we reach the carriage."

"Carriage?" Kitty asked, puzzled. "You've a carriage here?"

"Yes, I came to find you and take you away from here," he answered sternly. "Now come along before someone sees us."

As he urged her along, Kitty demanded, "How did you know I was here?"

Charles chose not to answer, for there were far too many people within earshot. Kitty would have repeated her question, but Charles squeezed her arm warningly, and although she bristled, she held her tongue until they reached the hack. Then the flood of questions came: "What are you doing here, Charlie? How did you know I was here? Does my aunt know? Do you think anyone could have recognized me?"

"I guessed you might have gone to the masquerade when Aunt Adele told me you claimed to have the headache," he answered coldly. "And Sara said she thought she had seen you with a green domino."

"How dare she tattle?" Kitty broke in hotly.

Charles answered bluntly, as the carriage lurched forward, "She was trying to help save your reputation, you ungrateful chit!" Then, abruptly, "Have you a ball dress under that domino?"

Puzzled, she said, "Yes, why?"

"Because I am taking you to Almack's."

"I don't want to go to Almack's!" Kitty said defiantly.

"Nevertheless, you will go," Charles retorted grimly. "You will say that you had the headache, and that I coaxed you out of it. Good God, girl! Have you no sense at all? How else can we hope to give the lie to gossip that you were at the Pantheon, if anyone should have recognized you?"

Biting her lip, Kitty gave in, and as soon as the carriage stopped, removed the domino to reveal her pink dress beneath. Charles was equally quick removing his domino. "A pity," he said, ruthlessly stuffing them under the cushions, "but we shall have to leave them. Can't walk into Almack's with them under our arms."

"But that was Mama's domino!" Kitty squealed in protest.

Sternly he answered, "You should have thought of that before you borrowed it."

It was precisely five minutes of eleven when the pair entered the portals of Almack's. Both Charles and Kitty were well aware that, once past the hour, nothing would have sufficed to gain them entrance. As it was, it seemed to Charles that Lady Jersey eyed them askance. To his dismay, she came over and

greeted them. "Good evening *again*, Major Farthingham! This is, I believe, your sister?"

"Yes, Miss Katherine Farthingham. She is making
her come-out in London with my aunt, Adele Farthingham," Charles said coolly.

Kitty seemed to visibly shrink under Lady Jersey's
appraising stare. Guessing at the Patroness's
thoughts, Charles added, "Kitty was to have come
with my aunt, but she had the headache earlier, so I
went to see her. You see, ma'am"—he lowered his
voice confidingly—"I leave London in the morning
and don't expect to see my sister again before I leave
for the Continent."

Lady Jersey seemed to be thawing, but nevertheless said bitingly, "I fail to see what that has to do
with your sister's headache."

Nobly Kitty stepped into the breach, saying
breathlessly, "Why, but Charles declared it a pity he
could not see me dancing, so of course I had to
come!"

Lady Jersey raised a slightly skeptical eyebrow,
but only waved them toward the dancing, saying,
"Then I must detain you no longer."

Sara, who had been watching from the far side of
the room, released the breath she had been holding,
as the formidable Patroness of Almack's moved away
from Kitty and Charles. She could see that several
other matrons stopped and quizzed the pair, but
Kitty seemed to have herself well in hand and was
able to laugh easily. Had Sara been close enough to
hear what was said, she must have been reassured,

for Kitty was replying that one could never refuse the commands of a military officer. It was enough. Kitty might be held to have been shamming her headache, earlier, but no one attributed this to anything graver than being a trifle spoilt.

Soon Charles appeared at Sara's side. She greeted him with a warm smile, saying, "Thank you, Charles! I collect you had no trouble?"

Charles, mindful of the eyes that were no doubt watching them, kept a smile, but his voice was serious as he briefly recounted what had occurred. He ended by saying, "We must trust no one recognized her. I have told Lady Jersey that Kitty recovered from her headache upon hearing this is my last night in town."

"Is it?" Sara asked in dismay.

Charles's smile was genuine as he replied, "Yes. I leave early in the morning, to go see my father. This time, I mean to obtain his consent to my marriage. Indeed, he will have no choice, for I must be off to the Continent within the next two weeks."

"I wish you good fortune," Sara said seriously. "Surely your father must relent when he sees how determined you are?"

"Let us hope so, though I place no such dependence on my mother's understanding. Now, I must go take leave of *your* mother; I've already stayed later than I intended."

Sara held out her hand to him. "I shall miss you."

Impulsively Charles raised her hand to his lips and kissed it. Then he was gone. Sara, smiling after him, suddenly became aware that the Earl of Danver was watching her. Meeting her eyes, Danver carelessly pushed his shoulders away from the wall that supported him, and came toward Sara. Her impulse was to flee, an impulse not lost on Danver. Abruptly he halted and smiled at her, maliciously. A moment later, Sara understood why, for Lord Scantham was at her side, bowing and begging for another dance. In spite of herself, Sara's eyes met Danver's, but he was, once more, leaning against the wall, watching with unmistakeable amusement. Unable to think quickly of a polite refusal, Sara found herself being led onto the dance floor. Fortunately, it was another country dance, and Sara was spared the need to make conversation as Lord Scantham concentrated on the figures of the dance.

Nevertheless, Sara could not but be pleased when the dance was ended. Until she realized that Lord Scantham showed no disposition to leave her side. Indeed, he appeared to be nerving himself to a declaration. This, perhaps, accounted for Sara's disproportionate relief at the appearance of Lord Danver, saying, as he did, "I believe I am promised this dance, Miss Farthingham?"

Sara gave him her hand, casting a falsely apologetic smile at Lord Scantham, who appeared alarmingly red at having his gallantries cut short. As the musicians began to play, however, Sara realized it was to be a waltz, and she gave a start of dismay. Feeling it, Danver tightened his hold on Sara and said in an amused undertone, "You did not bargain on the privacy of a waltz, did you, Miss Farth-ingham?"

Sara felt a moment of terror; then she had herself well in hand. Coolly she said, "I cannot conceive what you mean, my lord."

"No?" He was undoubtedly amused. "You are not afraid I shall ask awkward questions about your cousin?"

Sara laughed. "Charles? Why should you? You have already pressed upon me your views concerning him."

"I meant your *other* cousin," Danver retorted swiftly.

"Kitty had the headache," Sara replied, avoiding Danver's eyes as he smoothly guided their steps. "When Charles went to see her, she felt much better and begged him to bring her to Almack's."

Danver nodded and said seriously, "Yes, that should satisfy most of the tabbies."

Sara looked up at him in swift surprise. He was smiling down at her with oddly gentle eyes. Shaken, Sara heard him say, "I wish you would trust me, Miss Farthingham. You must know there is no need to fear that I would betray you or your cousins. I collect your cousin planned some folly, and her brother prevented it? Never mind, I shan't tease you anymore. I can guess that you feel it is your cousin Katherine's affair and that you ought not to speak of it to anyone."

Sara gave him a grateful smile, and, true to his word, Danver spoke of other, lighter matters. It was only as the last strains of the waltz were heard that he turned serious again. "Forgive me," he said, "but it seems that your cousin Charles is leaving now."

Sara was just in time to see the Major make good his exit from Almack's. "Yes," she told Danver. "He leaves in the morning, for his father's estate and hopes to make an early start, I collect."

Hearing something in her voice, Danver probed, "Does that disturb you?"

"If that were all," she answered, "then no. But soon after that, he leaves for Vienna, and I shall miss him."

By now the music had ended, and they were at the edge of the dance floor. Danver possessed himself of Sara's hand, and said, with quick sympathy, "I, too, must leave early. But if I can be of assistance, please believe I should wish to."

And then he kissed her hand, in the precise spot that Charles had. Before she could speak, Danver was gone, leaving Sara, and any number of jealous eyes, to watch his retreating back. Abruptly Sara became aware of those other eyes and straightened her shoulders. Foolish to refine too much upon the incident; impossible to pretend it did not matter to her.

Sara had little time, however, to dwell on such thoughts. Looking about the room, she saw an astonishing sight: Kitty standing up to dance with an elderly gentleman with whom they had not the slightest acquaintance! A rapid glance at the young men present showed Sara that Kitty's usual beaux were occupied with other young ladies. Before Sara could unravel the puzzle, *her* hand was solicited for the dance and she was obliged to turn her thoughts to polite conversation.

At least one other person was aware of Kitty's discomfort. Tom, however, had the advantage of *knowing* what was afoot, and when Kitty was returned to her place, on the side, by the elderly fellow, Tom was waiting. "M-m-may I have this dance, Miss Farthingham?" he asked stoutly.

Unhesitatingly Kitty said, "Yes!"

It was a waltz, and as they glided about the room, Tom asserted darkly, "*I* shan't desert you for a foreigner, no matter *how* pretty *some* people think her! Not even if she is the daughter of the Spanish Ambassador! And if anyone calls you spoilt in my hearing, I'll give 'em some of the home-brewed!"

It could not be said that Kitty was gratified by this speech. Indeed, her eyes sparkled in a way that Sara would unhesitatingly have characterized as dangerous. Kitty was not, however, entirely without sense, and she forced herself to smile at young Haverstock as she said lightly, "Has anyone deserted me? I hadn't noticed."

This tolerable assumption of composure was shattered by Tom's next words. "Of all the cork-brained things to say! So you ain't noticed, hey? Then why were you dancing with a fellow old enough to be your grandfather? Doing it much too brown, Kitty!"

Finding herself close to tears, Kitty retorted, "If you mean to be unkind, then I shan't dance with you."

At once, Tom was contrite. "Here! I say, Kitty! Don't *cry*. Didn't mean to upset you. Only meant to say you can trust me. Thought you'd be *grateful* for my support!" he ended on a distinct note of injury.

Hastily Kitty retrieved her smile. "Oh, I am, Tom!" she said meltingly. "It's only that everyone has been *so* unkind to me, and I was afraid you would be like the others, but I know, now, that you are not."

Under the warmth of Kitty's gaze, Tom began to look pleased with himself. He looked even more satisfied as the evening went on and Kitty granted him a third and then a fourth dance. Tom, who had never before been granted more than the prescribed two dances, must have been pardoned for feeling that, surely, Kitty was declaring her preference for him.

In truth, however, Kitty was bent more on punishing the other members of her court than on favouring Tom. Gradually, most of them drifted over to dance with her, but this could not be felt to atone for the slight they had shown her earlier. Nevertheless, Kitty greeted each of them with her dazzling smile, and no one guessed the turmoil in her breast. Only Sara might have understood the significance of her mood.

Adele certainly did not, when, emerging from the card room, sometime later, she collected her two charges. Greeting Kitty, she said, "My love, I am so pleased to see you have quite recovered from your headache. Charlie told me you had, and I confess I was vexed at the thought that perhaps you had not wanted to come and he had teased you to do it."

Kitty laughed and said, "Oh, no, Aunt Adele. My

headache quite vanished, after a short rest, and, indeed, I was delighted to have Charlie bring me."

"Good! Now, come along, my dears, our carriage will be waiting," Adele said, in happy ignorance of the evening's true events.

6

Lord Danver was riding, in the park, the next morning, when he encountered his friend Mr. Anthony Baffington. Reining in his horse, at Mr. Baffington's signal, Danver said, " 'Morning, Baffy! You're about early. Most unlike you."

With dignity, Baffy answered carefully, "Knew I'd find you here, at this hour. Wanted to warn you. Overheard your ward, Haverstock, bragging, last night—this morning . . . The devil, you know what I mean! Bragging about an engagement. Wanted to warn you. P'rhaps you know and it's none of my affair. Afraid maybe you didn't."

By this point, Danver was off his horse and face to face with Baffington. Grimly he demanded, "And who is Tom supposed to be engaged to? The Farthingham chit?" Baffy nodded, and Danver exclaimed,

"Damme! And where did my fool of a cousin make this announcement? Someplace public?"

"Cribb's Parlour," Baffy answered succinctly.

The Earl groaned. "It only wanted that! Well, tell me the worst: how many people heard?"

"Not many. But one fellow seemed devilish keen to spread the news. Be surprised if it ain't all over London by noon!" Baffy seemed genuinely distressed as he added, "Meant to catch you before you left your house. Knew I'd never make it. Dash it, can't tie a neckcloth in five minutes, you know!"

Danver clapped Baffy on the shoulder as he retorted, "You're a good friend, Baffy! And, believe me, I appreciate your sacrifice. I'll do what I can to scotch the rumours. Don't need to tell *you* what to say."

"I'll say the young cub had shot the cat. Didn't know what he was saying," Baffy said stoutly. Then he added gloomily, "Don't think it will help, though."

"We can only try," the Earl said grimly, as he remounted his horse. "Thanks for the warning, Baffy!"

Mr. Baffington's prophecy was soon proved correct. On his way out of the park, Lord Danver encountered no fewer than three of his acquaintances who made reference to young Haverstock's engagement. Danver parried the rumour, with a coolness he was far from feeling. He was also careful not to appear in too great a haste to leave the park. *That* could only have fueled the gossip further. Thus it was more than half an hour later when he reached Lady Haverstock's house. A curt query brought the information that both Lady Haverstock and Tom were still abed, and not to be disturbed, on any account. "I don't intend to disturb her ladyship," Danver said, proceeding up the stairs.

In the face of the Earl's determination, and in consideration of the fact that he had more than once been invited to run tame there, by her ladyship, the footman stood aside.

Tom's valet made one valiant effort to protect his master, but not unnaturally, in the end, decided that he preferred to face Tom's anger than my lord Danver's. Thus Tom was roused by an angry shake and a rough voice commanding him, "Wake up, damn you!"

Appalled, Tom opened his eyes to find Danver glaring down at him. Since Tom had been awake until close to dawn, drinking a trifle heavily, he found it a bit difficult to focus his mind and command his tongue. Nevertheless, he finally managed to say, "Ned! What o'clock is it? Feels like it's still before noon!"

"It *is* before noon!" Danver informed him unfeelingly.

This, naturally, aroused Tom's indignation. "Then what do you mean, bursting in on a fellow like this?"

A giggle, behind him, informed the Earl that he had forgotten to shut the bedroom door. He swiftly remedied the matter, dispersing the servants with a glare. Only then did he answer Tom's question. "What I mean is to discover the source of a rumour that I've heard, this morning, from several acquaintances. The rumour concerns *you!*" Danver paused to observe the effect on Tom, who appeared genuinely puzzled. Then, grimly, Danver went on, "Three of my acquaintances saw fit to offer congratulations on your engagement to Miss Kitty Farthingham!"

This enlightening pronouncement brought a look of dismay to Tom's face, and he groaned as he sat up hastily. Under his guardian's sardonic eyes, he flushed and stammered, "I . . . I . . . Oh, Lord, Ned!"

"I gather you have an explanation?" the Earl demanded.

Miserably, Tom held his head. "Don't shout, Ned! I've the devil of a head. It was because of Almack's. Kitty danced with me four times, and that must mean something, don't it? And then we were at Cribb's Parlour and I was sort of celebrating, and someone asked why, and—"

"And you said that you and Miss Farthingham were to be married?" Danver filled in abruptly.

Tom nodded. "Wrong thing to do, but I *was* under the hatches. Do you think Kitty will be very angry?"

Danver closed his eyes a moment before answering, "If she has the least bit of sense, she will be furious with you." Scathingly he added, "Even had the marriage contracts been signed, that would *not* have been the way to announce your betrothal!"

"Well, I know that!" Tom retorted indignantly. "Question is, what do I do about it?"

"First, I suppose you must see Kitty's father. I assume you *do* still want to marry her?" Danver waited only for Tom's assent before he went on, "Then you'll see Kitty, *if* her father approves your suit. *If* Miss Farthingham accepts, we shall make a formal announcement; otherwise, we shall do all in our power to scotch the rumour and make amends to Miss Farthingham. I suggest you leave, for the Farthinghams' estate, at once. I shall see the Farthingham ladies and see what comfort I may offer there."

Thus it was that, early that afternoon, John Farthingham was informed that a young gentleman had arrived, from London, to see him. He concluded, of course, that it was either a friend of Charles's or one of Kitty's suitors. "Show him in, Andrews," Farthingham said indulgently.

A few moments later, Tom entered the library, and his first words were an apology. "Forgive me, sir, for coming to you in my riding clothes, and dirt, but I didn't think to bring a change of clothes. I was rather in a hurry, you see."

These last words, and Tom's evident distress, brought a frown to John Farthingham's amiable face. "Oh? Would you care to sit down and explain?"

Tom flushed. "I think I should prefer to stand, sir." He hesitated, bit his lower lip, then plunged in. "I fear you are going to be angry, sir. It's about Kitty—Miss Farthingham, I mean. I've been rather indiscreet, you see."

Another man might have reacted with fury to the apparent implication of Tom's words. But John Farthingham was a sensible man, and he only replied, "I think perhaps you had better sit down. Good. Now, explain what you mean, if you please."

Tom did, leaving out nothing, including Lord Danver's opposition to the match. When Tom had finished, John said, "So your guardian opposed the match? Yet he sent you down here."

Stiffly Tom replied, "He is a man of honour."

"Quite." There was a pause. "Yes, I see. Well, I suppose we had best go to London and see Kitty."

"Sir?" Tom asked in confusion.

John Farthingham regarded Tom calmly. "I won't say I'm pleased, for that would be coming it too strong. Kitty's too young for marriage, and I wouldn't want it to be noised about, this way, in any event. Nor am I one to ignore a guardian's wishes. But I also know Kitty. It may be this match would be to her liking, and I've no wish to see her unhappy, and it seems to me that if you ain't to be engaged, you'll have to stop seeing her, altogether. So, we'll go to London and find out Kitty's mind." At the sight of Tom's woebegone face, he added comfortingly, "There, there, lad. To be sure, it was a very bad thing to do, but my Kitty is a fetching thing, and I can understand how you might have felt. Now, let me go inform my wife, and we shall set off for London, in the morning."

"The morning!"

"Aye, the morning," John confirmed dryly. "One day won't make so great a difference, and we shall be far more comfortable. Safer, too. Besides, I've a notion my wife will wish to make the acquaintance of the young gentleman who may become her daughter's husband."

Knowing his reception to have been far more cordial than he had had any right to expect, Tom had no choice but to agree. "Yes, sir." Then, hesitantly, "But I've brought no night things, and—"

"Precisely!" John chuckled. "Exactly the position *I* should find myself in, if I dashed off with you to London tonight. I should be certain to forget any number of essentials. Now, never mind about your night things, Haverstock. We can supply you with everything you need, I fancy. My son, Charles, is about the same build, and can lend you what you need. Became a regular Dandy, while he was in London."

"He's here?" Tom asked, astonished.

"Aye. Wanted to talk about marriage, too. Looks as though I may soon have only one child on my hands," he added jovially. Then, briskly, "Well, I shall send a note to my sister-in-law to inform her I'm coming. Would you like my man to carry a note to your guardian, as well?"

"Yes, thank you, sir."

John waved a hand. "No trouble, my boy. There. On that table, you'll find what you need. Now, I'm sure you'll excuse me while I go tell Fanny we've a guest."

Left alone, Tom hastily scribbled a note.

Ned,
    Have seen Kitty's father. Will stay the night and

arrive, together, in London, in the morning. Have permission to address Kitty.

                                        Tom

Charles Farthingham here, and apparently he means to be married, also.

The last line was added on impulse. Tom sealed the note and wrote his cousin's direction on the outside, wanting to be sure it would be ready when Kitty's father returned.

John Farthingham was finding the interview with his wife unexpectedly trying. "Haverstock. Not the highest-ranking of Kitty's suitors. However, Kitty did say this Haverstock is heir to an earldom," she said.

"Yes, but, Fanny, my dear," he noted dryly, "the Earl of Danver is not above thirty years old. I find it highly unlikely that he will remain unmarried and childless."

Fanny, who closely resembled her daughter, wrinkled her brow. "Oh. To be sure. Then you must refuse the boy."

John Farthingham bluntly explained the circumstances. Fanny was not impressed. "I don't care, John. Kitty can do far better for herself!"

For once, John Farthingham was firm with his wife. "Fanny, under any circumstances, my decision must be based on Kitty's feelings, *not* the status of her suitors, though, to be sure, I should prefer her not to marry someone altogether penniless."

"Feelings!" Fanny cried indignantly. "And what, pray, have they to say to anything? I was not asked *my* feelings when I was informed you had asked for my hand."

"We all knew your feelings," he answered dryly. "You were quite obvious in your *tendre* for that young army officer."

"Precisely!" Fanny confirmed. "And, as I recall, he was *quite* ineligible! So you see, there is not the slightest point in asking Kitty's feelings. After all, what could have been more felicitous than our marriage?"

John Farthingham, who was genuinely fond of his wife, did not answer. The years had taught him that a marriage of one-sided love could carry its own pain, its own price. For he had no illusion. Fanny might speak of their "marvelous" marriage, but in all these twenty-some years, she had never come to love him. All he said aloud, however, was, "Young Haverstock will stay the night, and he and I will leave for London in the morning." Before Fanny could protest further, he added, "I have already spoken with Mrs. Linden, and she tells me you are not to worry about a thing. She will manage all the necessary extra arrangements."

Fanny smiled wanly. "To be sure, it must be wonderful to enjoy such health as Mrs. Linden does. She is a most excellent housekeeper."

Closing the door to his wife's sitting room a few moments later, Farthingham could not entirely suppress a sigh. Charles, coming upon his father at that precise instant, looked at him quizzically. Bowing to the inevitable, John said, "Do you know Tom Haverstock, Charlie?"

Rather taken aback, Charles answered, "Yes. Why?"

"He's here. In the library. Come to ask for Kitty's hand."

"*What?*"

John explained, once more, the circumstances, and his own proposed course of actions. When he had done, Charles shook his head ruefully. "I'd best go join him in the library, then. And discover if there is anything he forgot to tell you!"

It took very little time for Charles to ease the story out of Tom, and to discover that Tom had been completely open with John Farthingham. Then it was Charles's turn to answer Tom's questions. "I shouldn't have asked about your plans," Tom explained shyly, "if your father had not spoken of the matter."

Charles smiled. "I plan to be married within the year, but first I hope to bring my fiancée's family to England."

"Oh? She's not English, then?"

"No. French. A refugee, now living with her family in Vienna." Almost unwillingly, he added, "My parents have finally consented."

Tom nodded in silent sympathy, then asked, "Have you sent in an announcement yet?"

"No. We plan to keep the matter private, for the moment." Noting Tom's stricken look, he asked, "Why?"

Miserably Tom indicated his note. "I . . . I mentioned it to my cousin, Lord Danver. But I can write the letter over again."

Charles regarded Tom with a mixture of exasperation and amusement. "Well, I have no real objection to Danver's knowing, but I should like the news to be otherwise kept quiet."

Relieved, Tom hastened to assure Major Farthingham, "You needn't worry, I shall be careful!"

"No doubt!" was the wry reply. Then, "Well, you'd best come upstairs to see if we can find you something suitable to wear for dinner. My mother's rather a stickler for proper dress, you know."

Charles's clothes did not quite fit Tom, but fortunately, Philip, John Farthingham's elder son, was also home and wore just the same size as Tom. Thus, Fanny, arriving to preside over the dinner table, found a most presentable young man waiting to pay his respects to her. Furthermore, the discovery that Tom had a family estate of his own, as well as being heir to the Earl of Danver, went a long way to reconcile Fanny to his suit. Charles, who already felt a certain amount of sympathy for Tom, sought to ease the ordeal of questioning by asking Tom if he had heard certain of the recent *on-dits* in London. This maneuver was heartily seconded by Philip, who, although he much preferred the country, could not deny a certain envy at his brother's experiences.

The meal was a rather simple one, Cook having had little warning. There were but three courses, with not above six or seven covers for each. Nonetheless, Tom pronounced it the best he had eaten in months. This could not fail to please John Farthingham, who prided himself on his reputation as a host who always set a good table. All in all, one might have said the meal passed off quite successfully.

Matters were not so happy at the Farthingham household in London. Adele had ventured forth that morning to exchange a book at the library and to run a few errands. She had been quite stunned when her particular friend, Mrs. Knollbridge, taxed Adele with not informing her of the "good" news. Good news? Katherine's engagement to young Haverstock. In great distress, Adele had attempted to refute the rumour. Nothing, she knew, could be more fatal to a young lady's chances than false rumours of that sort. She succeeded only in offending Mrs. Knollbridge. Leaving her errands undone, Adele fled home and immediately called for Kitty. Sara, of course, joined them.

"Katherine Farthingham," Adele began grimly, "have you contracted an engagement with Tom Haverstock, or anyone, without my knowledge?"

"Of course not!" Kitty said scornfully. "Why do you ask?"

"Because," Adele said frostily, "Amanda Knollbridge congratulated me this morning upon such an event. Wherever could she have gotten suth a notion?"

Neither Sara nor Kitty had the courage to tell her that Kitty had danced four times with Haverstock the night before. Furthermore, although such heedless conduct must cause certain matrons to censure Kitty, it scarcely seemed possible that it would give rise to such a rumour. Quietly Sara asked, "What shall we do?"

Adele threw up her hands helplessly. "What *can* we do, when even Amanda won't believe my denials? I suppose they must come from Haverstock or his guardian. I would give much to know who started the rumour!"

Hesitantly Kitty said, "Perhaps I've encouraged Tom's attentions too often."

Adele was thoughtful a moment before answering, "I think not. The rumour is far too firm to be based on mere speculation. No, for some reason, someone wishes you ill. Though why, I cannot imagine."

"You don't think, Mama," Sara suggested diffidently, "that Tom, himself, could have started the rumour?"

Adele was shocked. "Tom? Surely he would not be so lost to propriety!"

"Unless, perhaps, he were in his cups," Sara pointed out.

Again, Adele was thoughtful. "I'd best send a note requesting Lord Danver and Haverstock to call on us, for they must know of this gossip. I am sure it must dismay them as it does us."

"An excellent notion, Mama."

But, in the end, there was no need to send a note. With a fine disregard for the niceties, Lord Danver arrived at an hour when anyone else would have been sitting down to a nuncheon. Adele, Sara, and Kitty, however, were all quite willing to overlook this breach of social etiquette, in their gratitude for Danver's prompt appearance. When the Earl's name was pronounced, by a very disapproving Walthers, who knew what was due the ladies, even if they did not, Adele said, "Depend upon it! He has heard the rumours and come to reassure us!"

"Unless," Sara suggested dryly, "he has taken it into his head that *we* are responsible."

"Oh, no!" Adele exclaimed in lively dismay. "Surely he would not?"

At that precise moment, the Earl stepped into the Yellow Saloon. In his deep, quiet, cool voice he asked, "Surely I would not *what*, ma'am?"

Not unnaturally, this question threw Kitty and Adele into a confused silence. With a calm she was far from feeling, Sara said, "I must guess, Lord Danver, that you have heard the rumours concerning my cousin Katherine and your ward, Tom Haverstock." She paused and waited for him to nod before saying, "It was my fear that you might believe us to be the source of those rumours."

Lord Danver smiled, but his eyes were as cold as his voice. "No, I *know* the source of those rumours. My graceless ward, Tom! Indeed, I came to reassure *you*, in case you had heard them. I see that you have." Danver turned to stare at Kitty. "At this moment, Tom is on his way to speak with your father, Miss Farthingham. I expect him to return to London, today or tomorrow, with your father's permission to ask you to marry him."

"I won't marry Tom! I won't!" Kitty said emphatically. "Mama would never make me!"

"Kitty, please!" Adele remonstrated helplessly.

Surprisingly, it was Lord Danver who stepped into

the breach. Speaking coldly, he said, "Of course, if you do not wish for the match, there is nothing more to be said. You need only tell Tom your feelings."

"I shall!" Kitty interjected.

Unperturbed, the Earl went on calmly, "I must own, it is not a match *I* should look forward to, either. However, under the circumstances, Miss Farthingham, I should have suppressed my objections."

"What objections?" Sara demanded, rising to her cousin's defense.

"Why, the extreme youth of both parties, of course," Danver rejoined mildly. He waited politely for Sara to speak, and when it was clear she would not, he went on, "When Tom returns to London, and you have told him how you feel, Miss Farthingham, then we may discuss how best to refute the rumour and its ill-effects."

"Well, I must say, that is certainly very handsome of you," Sara said approvingly.

He smiled at her, then, his face transformed from forbidding to quite amiable. "Yes, isn't it?" he quizzed. "How fortunate no one else is here to see me say so. My reputation would be in shreds!"

Adele, unable to follow this exchange, but feeling as though they were treading on dangerous ground, made haste to say, "You must know, my lord, how excessively grateful we all are."

Danver merely bowed to her. Kitty, angry at being ignored, broke in to demand, "What I wish to know is how Tom came to do such a bird-witted thing?"

Recalling Tom's explanation of events, Danver retorted coldly, "Do you? I fancy you must already have guessed part of the answer, Miss Farthingham. Or am I wrong in believing that you were so indiscreet as to grant my ward no less than four dances at Almack's?" Her flushed face was sufficient answer for him, and he went on, "Did it not occur to you that such behaviour might lead my cousin to assume a warmth on your part that you now deny?" This time, he did not wait for an answer, but went on immediately, "Never mind, the damage is done. I only trust it will not prove irreparable." As he turned to Adele, his tone became less forbidding. "I will take my leave now. I realize this must seem an inconvenient moment for me to come by, but you see, I wished to be certain that you would not be entertaining morning callers."

"Oh, no! So kind of you to come at all!" Adele protested. Then, hesitantly, she asked, "When do you think we might look for Haverstock to call?"

"Morning," he replied decisively. "Even should he return tonight, he must be very late, and I believe he would put off the call until morning. With your permission, ma'am, I should like to return, tomorrow, to wait for him, also."

"I am sure we shall all be very grateful for your support, my lord," Adele answered warmly.

Once more, an engaging smile crossed the Earl's face, and then he bowed and left. As soon as he was gone, Adele Farthingham could not refrain from commenting on Danver's excessive civility and kind condescension. Finally, both Sara and Kitty fled to their rooms, on the pretext of preparing to sit down to a nuncheon. In truth, however, both young ladies felt that they could not bear to hear another word spoken in praise of the seventh Earl of Danver.

After the nuncheon, Adele and Sara considered the evening's invitations. Neither lady was so naive as to believe that the quandary would resolve itself, merely because Lord Danver had offered the Farthinghams his aid. Society still must be faced, and it would not be pleasant. Sara's immediate impulse, when asked about the evening's plans, was to say, "Cancel 'em, Mama, and stay home!"

Adele Farthingham, for all her other faults, had a sure sense for what one could or could not do, and she replied, horrified, "Oh, but, Sara, my love, you cannot have considered! If we stay home, then everyone shall say we are gone into hiding, and nothing would set matters right, not even if Kitty did consent to marry young Haverstock. (Not that I believe her father would agree to it, for John was always a most impractical man.) No, we must attend at least one of these events, but which one? Under other circumstances, I should have preferred Lady Farley's party, but she is sure to have heard the news, and she has the most uncanny knack of asking questions one cannot possibly answer truthfully. I simply cannot bear to face her tonight!"

"Very well, Mama," Sara said soothingly, "we need not consider Lady Farley's invitation. Shall we go to the Carthrops' ball, instead? *They* will be far too concerned with launching their daughter to be interested in gossip."

Rather mournfully, Adele agreed. "Yes, I suppose it must be the Carthrops', though I know I shall not enjoy myself! They always set such a shabby table, and no one cares, because their daughters are always such beauties!"

Suppressing an urge to laugh, Sara pointed out, "Yes, but no one said we were to enjoy ourselves; we are going in order to help Kitty."

With a deep sigh, Adele admitted the truth of this, and added, "One cannot blame the poor child for this, and I am sure no one could have guessed how it would be with young Haverstock, but I never looked for such trouble when I offered to sponsor Kitty for the Season!"

Sara smiled indulgently at her mother. "I know you did not. But confess it, life would have been very dull for us if you had not!"

Cheered by this reminder, Adele found herself beginning to look forward to the evening with rather less trepidation. Kitty, as might be imagined, was resolute in refusing to set foot outside the house, until matters had been resolved. Adele threw up her hands in disgust, and it was left to Sara to convince her cousin of the necessity of appearing at the Carthrop ball. In the end, she was successful, but exhausted.

Setting out that evening, Adele was resplendent in claret taffeta, Kitty was demure in white muslin, and Sara wore the sea-green that suited her so well. All three ladies had known, instinctively, that they would need the illusion of confidence that such clothes might give them. The Carthrops' ball was, at once, seen to be a deplorable squeeze. Moreover, the Carthrops themselves were far too preoccupied to pay any attention to the Farthingham ladies, once they had been greeted and heard to utter the appropriate compliments concerning Martha, a petite, dark-haired beauty with a flirtatious smile. As the Farthingham ladies moved away from the girl, Adele could not refrain from whispering to Sara, "I shall be much surprised, my love, if they do not have an announcement to make tonight, concerning Martha. I swear, it has become a tradition with them: set a date, mid-Season, for the girl's come-out ball, and announce an engagement at the same ball! Oh, well, it will serve us very well if they do, for depend on it, no one will have the least thought to spare for us."

This analysis may have been overly optimistic, but it was undeniably the case that the ladies were shielded more than they would have been at a smaller affair. Still, it was difficult. Kitty was forced to endure the humiliation of seeing her cousin Sara's hand solicited for the first dance, while she was forced to sit out. Fortunately, Sara's partner was an old friend, George Feathergill, and he was perfectly willing to carry out Sara's request that he ask Kitty to dance. Also willing were Sara's next three partners. After that, it was no longer necessary for Sara to make such requests. Seeing Kitty dancing with several different fellows, her court soon reappeared, if rather hesitantly, and Kitty was gratified to find herself dancing every dance, after the first one. She was well aware, however, that Sara's intervention had been necessary, and that her former suitors were still distinctly cooler to her this evening.

Adele, as befitted a chaperone, declined to dance

and spent much of her time carelessly laughing off rumours concerning Kitty and Tom Haverstock. She soon developed a horrid headache. The only fortunate circumstance, she felt, was that Tom could not be present, a circumstance that did not go unnoticed.

Sara was not quite so pleased at Lord Danver's absence. She knew, of course, that she should not have looked for him at such an affair; he was far more likely to be at cards, with friends. But Sara was conscious of a need to speak with him again, to have him reassure her that there was nothing to worry about. Nothing, at any rate, that could not be resolved. Uselessly, Sara chided herself for these missish thoughts, but it was impossible to banish them. Because she was a well-bred girl, however, none of this showed on her face, and she was able to return her partners' conversation with an easy smile, and a light reply.

What aided the Farthingham ladies the most, however, was the discovery that, for once, the Carthrops had no engagement to announce. As Martha was generally held to be the best, as well as the youngest, of the five Carthrop girls, this omission gave rise to speculation that quickly supplanted that concerning Kitty and Tom.

Nevertheless, it could not be other than a relief for Sara, Adele, and Kitty to descend from their carriage and mount the steps to the Farthingham house in Park Street. Walthers, alert to their arrival, was quick to place in Lady Farthingham's gloved hand the note that had been delivered in her absence. Recognizing, at a glance, her brother-in-law's writing, she exclaimed, "It's from John! Your father, Kitty. Depend upon it, he is writing to tell us he has seen Tom."

Sara, conscious of Walthers' intrigued expression, broke in to say, "Yes, well, let us go upstairs, Mama, and you can read it to us there."

"No need," Adele said, lifting her eyes from the note she had been perusing. "John merely writes that he is arriving tomorrow, before noon, for a brief visit. How odd, and just like him, to say no more."

Seeing Kitty's rebellious pout, Sara said hastily, "No doubt he means to tell us everything tomorrow. You may speculate, as you choose, but I, for one, am for my bed. Good night, Mama. Good night, Kitty."

Adele and Kitty quickly followed her example.

Lord Danver, on the other hand, did not seek his bed until some time later. He, too, upon returning home, found a billet waiting. It was, of course, the note from Tom. He read it hastily, without surprise, until he came to the postscript. This astonished him so much that he read the note a second time, and finally muttered. "The devil he is! Can I have been so mistaken, then?"

To his dismay, Danver realized that the answer mattered very much to him. He had not, until now, ever paused to analyze his feelings toward Miss Sara Farthingham. When he thought of her, it was to observe that he had seldom met a female with as much common sense as Miss Farthingham possessed, or a female who was so unafraid to match wits with him. It was, he thought, an attractive combination. Quietly Danver crumpled the note. If Tom's report were true, then he must, of course, be happy for Miss Farthingham, but it was rather a sense of emptiness that filled his thoughts as he slowly climbed the stairs to his room.

7

To the astonishment of the domestic staff, both Lady Farthingham and Miss Kitty joined Miss Sara at the breakfast table, at the unheard-of hour of eight A.M. Only Sara, however, looked as if she had slept. Kitty's eyes were red-rimmed and dark, and Adele betrayed her fatigue by the droop of her shoulders, under her morning shawl. Barely repressing a shudder, Adele said to Sara in a taut voice, "How can you be so *unfeeling* as to speak to me of *eggs* at this hour? A bit of toast and tea is all I shall be able to swallow, and only because I must."

Sara merely nodded calmly, and turned to Kitty, saying, "Shall you also be fasting?"

But Kitty was too young to be so affected. She greeted the suggestion with scorn, saying, "Of course not! I shall have my usual breakfast." Pausing, she sniffed, "I see *your* appetite is unimpaired also, Sara. But then, it is not your future at stake!"

Sara poured her mother a cup of tea before replying, "I am not unconcerned, Kitty. However, I cannot conceive what use it would be for me to starve myself. Or, indeed, to allow myself to become overwrought."

This bracing response had its effect on Adele, who straightened her shoulders and said, "Well, perhaps I might attempt an egg, after all. It is of primary importance that we should recruit our strength."

Sara betrayed, only by the slightest easing of the tension in her carriage, the relief she felt. She loved her mother dearly, and respected her for those excellent qualities she possessed, but fondness did not blind her to her mother's faults. Nor to Kitty's. She was not surprised, therefore, when Kitty demanded petulantly, "I wonder when they shall arrive? I *won't* marry Tom, you know, and I shall tell my father so, at once!"

Helplessly Adele said, "Well, of course you need not, if you don't wish to, my dear, but I can't help feeling that you ought to be gentle with the poor boy."

Sensing a storm about to burst, Sara cut in hastily, "Yes, yes, we have been through all this before, and I see no need to spend all our time, between now and your father's arrival, Kitty, discussing it again. Please let us talk of something else!"

It was not to be expected that this sensible reply would find favour with Kitty, and it did not. However, as Kitty's response was to pout silently, Sara could not be altogether sorry she had offended her cousin. She strongly felt that this was one morning she simply could not endure Kitty's outbursts. Indeed, Sara wished very much for a solitude she was certain she would not be allowed.

Her fears were soon confirmed. Shortly after breakfast, Sara said quietly, "I think I shall attend to the accounts, Mama."

"Oh, no, Sara!" Kitty protested. "How can you be so unfeeling? You must know I need you by me!"

Too well-bred to own her impatience, and too good-natured to remain unmoved by Kitty's distress, Sara reseated herself and said, "All right, Kitty."

The three ladies busied themselves with their needles, with varying degrees of skill. None of them, however, was sorry when, promptly at eleven o'clock, Walthers announced Lord Danver. "Show him up at once," Adele directed, with only the slightest quaver in her voice.

As he entered the Yellow Saloon, Lord Danver bowed to Adele, saying, "Good morning, ma'am. I trust you have also received word that your brother-in-law and my ward are to arrive this morning?"

Adele nodded. "Yes, and I am grateful to you for coming."

Danver then disconcerted her by shrugging. He was, in fact, more interested in speaking with Sara, who had unaccountably fled to the window. Casually he strode over to stand beside her. "Watching for them, Miss Farthingham?" he asked quietly.

"Just so, my lord," Sara answered with a smile.

The Earl hesitated, then said, with a careless calm

he was far from feeling, "Tom writes me that your cousin Major Farthingham is also planning to be married?"

Sara felt her colour rising and hastily lowered her eyes. In a small voice she said, "You cannot expect me to speak of that, my lord."

The Earl swore, under his breath. "Sara, look at me! I—"

Alarmed by her own reaction to his nearness, Sara turned away instead, saying loudly, "Perhaps we should ring for a tea tray, Mama?" Behind her, Sara could hear Danver swearing, once more, and she added quickly, "Never mind, I shall go myself. Indeed, I forgot to speak to Cook about supper, and you must know how particular my uncle is."

Before anyone could stop her, Sara was gone from the room. Adele, gazing after her helplessly, tried to apologize to the Earl. "I'm very sorry, my lord. In general, Sara is such an amiable girl!"

"You need not be distressed, ma'am," Danver said coolly. "I quite understand."

In the face of the Earl of Danver's aloof composure, Adele had no alternative but to fall silent. Nor would she have been reassured, had she seen Sara pausing, halfway down the stairs, to regain her poise, but Sara felt it unthinkable that the servants should be allowed to see her so flustered.

When Sara did finally return to the Yellow Saloon, it was in the wake of the maid who carried a tray of refreshments. Having delayed said return until she heard the sounds of her uncle's arrival, Sara was not in the least surprised to see him, or Tom, there also.

Dutifully she said, "Good morning, Uncle John. How was your journey?"

"Sara, my dear, how are you?" he asked, kissing her cheek.

John Farthingham was genuinely fond of his niece Sara. Indeed, he had often, secretly, wished that she might have been his daughter, instead of Kitty. To his mind, Sara's gentle intelligence was far more desirable a quality than Kitty's shallow beauty, though it must, in fairness, be added that John Farthingham doted on his daughter. Nonetheless, Sara's visits to his estate had always delighted John, for she could converse with him, in the sensible, well-informed way that Kitty and Fanny never could.

Adele interrupted the pair, with her slightly shrill voice, to say, "Sara! Only fancy, John tells us Charlie is to be married!"

Conscious of the eyes on her, Sara looked at her uncle. "Indeed, sir? I had thought you set against it." Then, very softly, in case she might be mistaken, she added, "Lisette?"

Loudly John confirmed, "Aye, Lisette. And you're right, my dear, I have opposed Charlie's marriage, before this. But he's convinced me that the attachment is genuine."

Sara smiled. "I'm glad, sir. I also believe the attachment to be sincere, and I believe he shall be happy with her."

John smiled back and, in an altered tone of voice, said, "Well, now, I think we'd best sort out this marriage business here. Has that maid left? Yes? Good. Sit down, everyone, sit down!"

In spite of his words, John Farthingham remained standing. When everyone else was seated, he addressed his daughter. "Now, Kitty, young Haverstock, here, has come and explained the circumstances to me and, very properly, asked permission to pay his addresses to you. What do you say, my dear?"

"I won't marry him! I won't!"

John Farthingham raised his hands. "All right, Puss. No one intends to force you. Calm down." Turning to Tom, he said, "Well, there's your answer. Now, what's to be done?"

Tom was staring at the floor, an angry flush on his face. Slowly the Earl of Danver stood up. "Perhaps it would be best," he said mildly, "to ascertain *precisely* what was said, and how far the damage may have spread."

"As to that," Adele bristled, "I am sure it has spread much too far! I cannot begin to count the number of acquaintances who have presumed to congratulate me on the news of Kitty's engagement!"

Coolly Danver cut her short, "Fortunately, ma'am, no one is asking you to count them." This, not unnaturally, silenced the poor lady, and Danver turned again to Tom. "Can you recall your exact words, Tom?"

Tom frowned with the effort to concentrate. Finally he said, "I . . . I was in my cups, Ned. A trifle foxed. But I believe I said . . ." He hesitated, then began again. "George Pomroy said that Miss Kitty Farthingham clearly seemed to be favouring my suit. Well, Fitz Hathcart—you've seen him, Ned, a loose fish, if there ever was one—sneered and said I was puffing off empty wishes. I . . . I lost my temper, then, and said, 'That's all you know! You may expect to see, soon, an announcement of a very interesting connection between her family and mine!' I know it was wrong of me, Ned, but—"

Danver cut him short. "Are you quite sure those were your *exact* words?" When Tom nodded, Danver said thoughtfully, "And what was the reaction?"

Gloomily Tom replied, "Hathcart laughed and said, 'An engagement, I suppose? I would as soon expect your cousin, the Earl of Danver, to announce his wedding, as hear that Miss Kitty Farthingham is to marry you!'" No one noticed Kitty's unnatural pallor, at the mention of Hathcart's name, as Tom added, "Well, of course I refused to answer him, and that was that. Except that my friend Pomroy took up the cudgels, in my defense, and insisted that if I said there was to be an announcement, then there would be an announcement."

As Tom's words died away, an unfortunate silence settled over the occupants of the Yellow Saloon. Finally, after a good many minutes, Danver said, "I should say the only solution is to make an announcement."

At this, Kitty was on her feet, facing Lord Danver, her fists clenched. "I won't marry Tom, do you hear me? I won't!"

Danver regarded her mildly. "Calm yourself, child. I never said you should. I meant an announcement of *my* engagement."

For a moment, there was a stunned silence. Then Sara's sensible voice asked the inevitable question,

"Yes, but Tom said the announcement was to concern your family and mine. How will you deal with that?"

With maddening composure, the Earl said, "I meant, of course, my engagement to Miss Sara Farthingham."

Stunned again, Sara could only stare at him as, around her, the others all started throwing questions.

"By Jove, that would do it!" Tom cried.

"My love, why didn't you tell me how matters stood?" Adele asked her daughter joyfully.

"How could you be so sly?" Kitty demanded of her cousin. "Not a word to us!"

Only the Earl and John Farthingham were as silent as Sara. John studied both faces before saying, as the other voices finally died away, "Well, Sara, how do you feel about this? Is it what you want? If not, you need only say so, my dear, and no one shall force you."

Sara looked first at her uncle, then unwaveringly at the Earl. "I'm afraid Lord Danver must have been joking. It's quite impossible, of course."

"Why?" Danver demanded abruptly.

Helplessly Sara said, "You must see how absurd it all is?"

John Farthingham, still watching both faces closely, drew his own conclusions. To Danver he said, "This was a damn-fool place to propose, you know. (No, Adele, I won't apologize for my language.) My lord, why don't you and Sara discuss this alone, in the library?" Turning to Sara, he went over and took her hands and said gently, "Go with him, my dear. I promise you, no one shall force you into anything, but you cannot possibly consider Lord Danver's offer in the middle of all this madness!"

Meeting her uncle's eyes, Sara forced a smile. "Very well, sir."

John held the door as the two walked out: Danver calmly, Sara stiffly, her chin held high. Then, as he closed the door behind them, Farthingham turned to his sister-in-law and said, "Well? Is it impossible to get a glass of port in this house?"

To call the small room whose walls were lined with overcrowded bookshelves a library was to accord it a dignity it did not truly possess. Nevertheless, it did house the family books, as well as a desk for settling accounts, bills, and so forth. It also boasted a small fireplace and two windows. It was to one of these windows that Sara immediately fled, bracing herself for Danver's first words. When they came, however, they astonished her into turning around to face him. "Good God!" he ejaculated. "What on earth possessed your father to cram his books into such an obviously unsuitable room, when there are surely other rooms in this house better suited to the purpose?"

In spite of herself, Sara laughed. "I quite agree with you, sir, it *is* appalling. But my father did not choose to clutter up, as he put it, any of the other rooms, with anything so unessential as *books*! Indeed, he said that this was the very room for them, as it was far too small for any comfortable use anyway."

"But you do not agree?" Danver asked.

"No, I do not agree." Sara sighed, unaware that she had done so. "I love these books, and would give them a room four times this size, with comfortable chairs, if I could."

"When you are my wife, you shall order the Danver library in any way that you choose," he promised.

Feeling hunted, Sara replied, "You must not speak nonsense, my lord! We are not going to be married."

"Why?" was the uncompromising reply.

Sara decided on honesty. "You do not care for me and I . . . I . . ."

Danver's voice was firm as he said, "And you have just received a blow. Your cousin Major Farthingham is to marry someone else."

Sara lifted her head and said coldly, "You are mistaken. It was not a blow but, indeed, good news. I have, for some time now, been expecting such an announcement."

In exasperation, the Earl strode forward and possessed himself of Sara's hands. "Don't try to bamboozle me, girl! I know very well how you feel! Now, tell me why you won't marry me. It will resolve your cousin's problem, and you are not attached to anyone else, are you?"

Feeling her colour rise and her senses betraying her, Sara could only trust herself to shake her head. Seeing this, Danver went on roughly, "What is it, then? Am I so distasteful to you? Is it my lack of manners or confounded temper? Are you afraid I shall be too strict a husband? I promise you, you shall do as you wish."

With an effort, Sara pulled her hands free and turned to face out the window. Her hands gripping the window ledge tightly, she schooled her voice to steadiness as she said, "Why are you asking me to marry you, my lord?"

As her back was to him, Sara could not see Danver's face, otherwise she might have had her answer. But she did not, and it was several moments before he answered, with tolerable composure, "It is time I had a wife, and this will help to solve your cousin's problem, and ... well, why not?"

Sara bit her lower lip, desperately searching for the strength to refuse Lord Danver. But, in the end, she said, turning to face him and offering him her hand, "If you are sure, sir, then I accept."

Slowly, his eyes searching her face, Danver took her hand and said, "You shan't regret it, I promise you."

Swiftly Sara lifted her eyes to his. "My fear is that *you* shall be the one to regret it!"

Danver smiled down at her reassuringly, but only said, "Come. We ought to inform your family."

It was not to be expected that Sara's family would share, in view of the brilliant nature of the match, her trepidation. And, indeed, after listening with amazement as Lord Danver made the announcement, Adele and Kitty crowded around Sara, hugging her. Meanwhile, Tom heartily congratulated his cousin. Only John Farthingham hung back, again studying faces. Apparently he was satisfied, for he joined Tom in saying to Danver, "Congratulations." Then he added, "I think very highly of my niece, my lord, and I hope I may trust you to take care of her as she ought to be taken care of? For I warn you, I shouldn't countenance the match, otherwise, even if you are an earl!"

Gravely Danver replied, "I shall, indeed, take good care of her, sir."

Farthingham then went over to speak with Sara, and she found it difficult to meet his eyes. But when she did, she found they held only warm understanding. Impulsively she hugged him, and gently he patted her back, saying soothingly, "There, there, girl. He seems a good enough man."

A few minutes later, Tom and Lord Danver took their leave. The former to return home and the latter to draft a formal announcement to send to the papers. When they were gone, Sara inexplicably burst into tears. Immediately, Adele was by her side asking, "My love, what's wrong? Is it Lord Danver? You do wish to be engaged, don't you? For, if you do not, I daresay there is still time to send someone after him and prevent the announcement."

Kitty also was distressed. "Oh, Sara! Did you do it for me? You need not have, if you dislike it so much!"

Only John Farthingham remained unperturbed. Sara, raising her face from her hands, found him watching her calmly. That was enough to steady Sara, and she said, with creditable composure, "You must forgive me, Mama, I can't think why I should have reacted like this. Of course I wish for the engagement. I think it is only that my nerves are a bit overset."

Adele nodded, as though this were only to be expected, as perhaps it was, then confided, "I thought that you might not quite like it, but for my part, I have always found Lord Danver excessively amiable, and I cannot but be pleased at the notion of my daughter as a countess."

Kitty, quiet too long, broke in, "When is the wedding to be, Sara? Aren't you excited? They say he has *four* estates, and the largest has an abbey!"

"Yes," John Farthingham said, speaking finally, "when *is* the wedding to be?"

Looking at him, with some surprise, Sara said, "I don't know. We didn't speak of it."

"When are you going to see him again?" Kitty demanded.

Again the reply was, "I don't know." Then, before she could be besieged with any more questions, Sara rose, a bit unsteadily, to her feet, and said, "I believe, Mama, Uncle John, Kitty, I shall go lie down for a bit, before luncheon."

That brought Adele to her feet, also. "An excellent notion, my love. And you need not come down to luncheon unless you choose. Betsy can bring you a tray, and I am sure it is no wonder that you wish for quiet. Why, when my father told me *your* father had asked permission to marry me, I took to my room for two whole days!"

As none of Adele's listeners quite knew how to reply to this, Sara was able to leave without any further comment. Reaching her room, however, was not such a simple matter. Clearly, the servants had somehow gotten wind of the matter, and it seemed to Sara that the entire staff had managed to congregate, on the route to her bedroom, in order to congratulate her. There was no doubt that the congratulations were sincere, either, for Sara was quite a favourite with the staff, and more than one was heard to say that it was only right Miss Kitty should not have all the beaux, that Miss Sara's engagement should come first.

So it was that Miss Sara, upon reaching her room, felt totally exhausted, and Betsy, looking in, with a tray, an hour later, found her sound asleep. Quietly Betsy withdrew to the kitchen, to inform the others that Miss Sara needed her rest.

The Earl, unwilling and unable to take similar refuge in his bedroom, sought his library, instead. A room which instantly conjured up Sara Farthingham's face. Lord Danver rang for his secretary, and dictated the formal announcement of his betrothal. He was then forced to endure the fellow's astonished congratulations before he could be alone again. And when he was, the Earl found himself wondering what he had done. It was not, precisely, that he regretted asking Miss Sara Farthingham to marry him. It was more, perhaps, that he had not married her out of hand and avoided all the fuss attendant to engagements and weddings in his stratum of Society. Well, there was no choice now. As a man of honour, he certainly could not draw back from the betrothal, nor, he was sure, could he ever persuade sensible Miss Farthingham to elope.

Oddly enough, the least disturbing facet of the situation was the notion of being leg-shackled, a tenant-for-life. He couldn't have said just when the change had occurred, but Lord Danver found himself almost anticipating the sight of Sara presiding over his table, or accompanying him to Paris. There were other, more intense images that passed through the Earl's mind, but he was well aware that he would need to go slowly with so gentle and wellbred a young lady as Sara. Particularly as Danver could not deny that she came to him somewhat reluctantly. A shadow crossed his face then, but he shook it off roughly, telling himself that he should be a poor sort of fellow if he could not make Sara forget her cousin.

Two glasses of excellent port later, Lord Danver decided to go to White's and see his friends Tiverton and Baffington. He tugged the bell pull, only to recall his mother. *She* would need to be informed of the engagement *before* the news appeared in print. A footman, Peters, appeared, only to be informed, roughly, that he was not needed, after all. Recognizing one of Lord Danver's black moods, the fellow hastily retreated to the kitchen, where the servants had gathered to discuss the news of his lordship's betrothal. Not having been requested to keep the matter confidential, Danver's secretary had naturally spoken of it to James, the butler, who had not disdained to repeat it to the chef. Until Peters returned from the library with the account of the Earl's dark mood, everyone had naturally assumed the tidings to be happy ones. Peters' information, however, placed the matter in another light, for, as he said, "Stands to reason, don't it, that if 'is nibs wanted to be riveted, he'd be looking happier, now, wouldn't he?"

Peters was, of course, immediately hushed by his superiors, but most of the servants felt there was a certain truth in what he said. Feeling began to run high against the unknown Miss Sara Farthingham, until Danver's valet entered the fray. Coughing discreetly, he said, "Well, now, as to that, I'm not generally one to gossip, but being, as one might say, in a privileged position to his lordship, I think I can say, with certainty, that whatever has distressed his lordship, it was *not* Miss Sara."

This, not unnaturally, changed matters, and opinion now ran in favour of the young lady, Mrs. Watkins going so far as to say it would do his lordship good to have a pretty face to come home to. She *was* pretty, wasn't she?

Here it was that Timothy came into his own, being one of the very few privileged to have seen her. Taking his time, he said judiciously, "Well, as to that, one wouldn't call 'er pretty, exackly. Not one of those flighty bits of fluff one sees about. She 'as dignity, she 'as, and a werry fine counternance, and *I* think she'll suit 'is lordship perfeckly!"

Oblivious of the furor his announcement had caused belowstairs, Lord Danver sealed the letter to his mother, then prepared to set out, on foot, for White's. It was an unusually fine day, a fact which rapidly restored the Earl's good humour. He would, he decided, spend the evening at cards with his friends Sir Frederick Tiverton and Mr. Anthony Baffington. They were not difficult to find, having, as usual, set themselves near one of the bow windows. "Hallo, Freddy, Baffy!" he greeted them cheerfully.

"Ned! Good to see you. Try some of this claret. Devilish fine!"

Mr. Baffington was more reserved. " 'Afternoon, Ned. What news?"

"News?" Danver grinned. "Why, only that I have just become betrothed to Miss Sara Farthingham."

Both Tiverton and Baffy goggled at him, unable to speak. Danver, obviously aware of their shock, suddenly found his courage deserting him. "Must go," he said hastily. "Just wanted you to know."

"Hey! Here, wait!" Tiverton called after him, but the Earl had already gone.

Danver could not have said precisely why he fled his friends. He only knew that their reaction was a foretaste of what he might expect as the rest of the *ton* heard the news. Once more, Danver sought refuge in his library to consider what he had done.

8

Early the next morning, Sara and her uncle, John Farthingham, had breakfast together, alone. Neither Kitty nor Adele was yet awake. At first, they talked of inconsequential matters. Then, his perceptive gaze on her, Farthingham asked, "Is this betrothal what you wish, Sara? A night's reflections have not changed your mind?"

Sara hesitated, then answered frankly, "No, I have not altered my opinion. I know this engagement must seem a trifle unconventional to you, Uncle John, but I do wish for it."

She stopped, unaccountably shy, and Farthingham nodded. "Aye. You've a *tendre* for him, I know. Well, my dear, I don't say this is the way I would like to see things arranged for you, for it's my belief you ought to have been courted properly, but it's also my belief his lordship is a good fellow and the match not such a bad one."

Sara could not help laughing at her uncle's judicious tone. Dryly she said, "No, the match can scarcely be said to be a *mean* one, can it? You are roasting me, sir! I am well aware what a matrimonial prize I shall be said to have snared!" She paused. "My only concern, sir, is that Lord Danver will regret the match."

John Farthingham regarded his niece kindly. "His lordship seems quite capable of knowing his own mind, I should say, and in my opinion, the two of you will make the marriage work. Good Lord, child, neither of you wants for sense!"

"Unless," Sara countered, with a chuckle, "you would call his offer of marriage to me a great piece of folly!"

John laughed. "You can hardly expect me to say that, when you know very well you're my favourite niece and that I think you far too good for any *mere* earl!"

Sara's good sense, retrieved by her uncle's easy humour, allowed her to rise from the table in measurably higher spirits. She excused herself, saying, "Betrothal or no, I *must* tally the accounts. I can't imagine what Mama will do about them, when I am gone."

Irresistibly, Farthingham retorted, "No doubt she will bring them to you, every quarter, for you to settle."

Their eyes met in perfect understanding, and Sara laughed as she left for the library. She was still there, working on the accounts, when the door of the room opened, sometime much later. Assuming it was Kitty or her mother, Sara set down her pen with a sigh. At once, a deep voice asked, with concern, "Do I disturb you?"

Sara's head snapped up as she gasped, "Lord Danver!"

Ruefully he advanced, holding out his hands, in a gesture of surrender. "I must beg your pardon. Your butler assured me you were to be found here, and that you would not mind the interruption. Shall I go away?"

"No! That is, there is not the slightest need." Sara broke off in confusion. She was intolerably aware of how fine he looked in dove-coloured pantaloons and a coat of blue superfine. His neckcloth was tied in the Mathematical, and his locks brushed *coup du vent*.

The Earl, for his part, was highly conscious of Sara's curls, framing her face so charmingly, and the pale green muslin dress that suited her figure so admirably. Nor could he be displeased by the blush that coloured her cheeks. By now, he was at the desk, and, glancing down, he saw the papers she had been working on. "Good God!" he exclaimed involuntarily. "Accounts?"

Sara's ready sense of humour came to her rescue, and she was able to quiz him, saying, "Alas, my secret is out! You have betrothed yourself to a *bluestocking*!"

As this last was spoken in tragic accents, Danver's mouth began to quiver, and he retorted, "Ah, but I was forewarned! You betrayed yourself over the library. What *you* didn't know is that I propose to have you handle all *our* accounts, once we are wed."

Diverted, Sara asked, "Really? But you don't know whether I can. Tally correctly, I mean. Papa never let Mama near the accounts."

"Nor shall I allow you near them," Danver replied, turning serious. "Whatever possessed your father to teach you to keep them?"

"He didn't," Sara answered frankly. "I began looking them over, out of curiosity. However, when Papa discovered me, his only comment was to say that I was hopeless anyway!"

"Well, he could say so no longer," Danver retorted. "The formal announcement of our betrothal will appear in a day or so. I daresay no one will then venture to call you hopeless."

Sara laughed. "No, they will say I am odiously scheming, and I shall be given the cut by any number of jealous mamas."

"And when you are countess, you shall give them the cut!" Danver retorted.

"No, how could I?" Sara protested, with a smile. "I should be sadly wanting in conduct, if I did so!"

Danver smiled down at her and said, "How shocking that would be! But think of how much fun."

"Are you never serious?" Sara asked, her eyes still dancing.

He paused; then, abruptly serious, he said, "Sometimes. Sara, I know this engagement is not quite what you wanted, but I think we shall deal well together. In time, you will forget your cousin, I promise you."

"You mistake the matter," Sara said softly. "There is nothing to forget."

To her surprise, he nodded approvingly. "Good girl. I'm glad to see you've found your pride. No! I won't quarrel with you, Sara. I've already sent in the notice of our engagement, and I couldn't bear the humiliation of a retraction!"

The gentle amusement in his voice robbed the words of their offensiveness, as did the smile he gave her. Danver paused and looked about the room, then said, "I should like you to see the library at Swinford Abbey. Indeed, I should like you to see all of the Abbey. Will you come, for a week or two? It will be a small house party. You, your cousin, your mother. Myself and my mother. Perhaps one or two of my friends. I shall speak to your mother, of course, but I want to be sure you like the notion. I've no desire to ride roughshod over you, now or ever."

Sara found it impossible to resist asking innocently, "Do you mean to say I shall have my way, in all things?"

Danver grinned down at her appreciatively. "Baggage! I have no intention of allowing you to ride roughshod over me, either, my girl!"

Sara laughed. Then, shyly, "I should like very much to visit Swinford Abbey."

"Good. Then leave your accounts, and we'll go find your mother and ask her consent to the scheme. Then I intend to take you riding, my girl. It's too fine a day to spend indoors working on your accounts!"

"Riding roughshod over me already, my lord?" Sara quizzed him.

He laughed. "Just so. And you might call me Edward, you know. In view of our betrothal, I cannot think it would be *improper*."

Colouring, she managed to say, "Very well. Edward." Then, collecting herself, she added briskly, "Shall we go find my mother? I am sure she must be in the Yellow Saloon."

She was. As were Kitty and her father. All three looked up, with no little surprise, as Sara entered, followed by the Earl. "Walthers showed Lord Danver to the library," she explained ruefully.

The Earl took over then, addressing Lady Farthingham. "I came to ask, ma'am, if you and your daughter and your niece would consent to form part of a small house party at Swinford Abbey. My mother will be there, of course, and you, sir, if you would care to come."

A night's reflection had sufficed to convince Kitty that Sara's betrothal could only add to her, Kitty's, consequence, and now it occurred to her that a brief removal from London, to visit the Earl's estate, might be the very thing to bring round her beaux again. She, therefore, greeted Lord Danver's proposal with eager approval. "Oh, Aunt Adele, say we may go!"

Adele cast a reproving glance at her niece before replying, "We would be delighted, my lord."

Danver gave her one of his rare smiles then, and

turned to John Farthingham. "Will you come, also, sir?"

He shook his head. "No, I'll be returning home to-day."

"Must you?" Sara asked, with genuine regret.

"Aye," he said seriously, "I hope to slip out of London without anyone knowing I've been here. For you must know that *my* presence would only lend credence to the rumours concerning Kitty."

"Unless they felt you had come to town so that Lord Danver could speak to you about Sara," his sister-in-law suggested.

John raised a questioning eyebrow at Sara, who retorted, "Come, Mama, I am of age! And I've no wish to be known as a Bath miss who must consult her uncle before accepting an offer!"

"But it would be considered a most dutiful and proper thing to do!" her mother protested. "Do you mean to say you don't wish your uncle to accompany us?"

Stricken, Sara turned to her uncle. "Indeed, sir, that wasn't what I meant. I should be most pleased if you did go with us."

John smiled at his niece, fondly. "I know what you meant, my dear. And I cannot but feel that my presence *would* lead to gossip about my Kitty, for though I might be considered to be here on *your* be-half, in view of the recent rumours, it is far more likely that I had come because of young Tom. And that is precisely the gossip we most wish to avoid. Don't you agree, my lord?"

Danver nodded soberly. "Unfortunately, I do, but

I must regret that you cannot be one of the party."
Sara smiled gratefully at him, and he returned the
smile before saying to Adele, "Thank you for con-
senting, ma'am. And now, if you will permit me, I
shall bear Sara off for a drive."

Naturally, Adele permitted it, and the pair was
soon gone, leaving the other three to their delightful
conjectures.

Much later that day, Lord Danver could be seen
entering White's. He quickly found his friends Sir
Tiverton and Mr. Baffington, seated where they had
been the day before. That they had been discussing
him was obvious from the way they broke off their
conversation at the sight of him. Laughing, Danver
settled his tall frame into a chair and said, "Think I
should be clapped up in Bedlam, don't you? Well,
Freddy, you've had a night to think about it. Anything to say today?"

Stoutly Tiverton said, "I wish you happy, Ned.
Miss Farthingham is a sensible young woman and
should make you an admirable wife. I'm delighted
for you."

With an engaging smile, Danver retorted, "No,
you're not, Freddy, you're appalled! You hadn't the
faintest notion anything like this was afoot. And, in
any case, you never looked to see me leg-shackled at
all, I'll wager!"

Baffy startled them both by saying, "Think it will
answer very well, Ned. Mind you, it's a trifle extreme, but there it is. All the better. Tabbies will
speak of nothing else, for weeks."

Sir Frederick Tiverton stared at his friend in astonishment. "Have you gone *mad*, Baffy? What the deuce are you talking about?"

"Never mind," Danver told Tiverton soothingly. Then, to Baffy, amused, "Do you think that's the reason I did it? I hope you may be the only one who does."

Baffington shifted his weight slightly before answering judiciously, "Must be. No one else would believe it." Then, in alarm, "No, Freddy! No use popping me one! Shan't explain. Ask Ned, if you must." Then, again, to Danver, "Seen the girl. Talked with her once. Very sensible. Probably have a good head at cards. Yes, I think it will answer very well indeed."

Refusing to answer Tiverton's indignant questions, Danver stood up and strolled away, saying he needed to find young Haverstock.

Haverstock was busy discussing neckcloths with a friend. At the sight of Lord Danver, he broke off and cried, "Ned! There you are. George says there's to be a mill next week. Care to go?"

"Hullo, Tom, Mr. Pomroy. Sorry to disoblige you, Tom, but I shall be at Swinford Abbey." Danver turned to Tom's friend and explained, "I am taking my fiancée to visit my ancestral home."

The fellow gaped at Danver. "Fiancée? *You*?" Then, hastily, "Mean to say, wish you happy! Should have told me, Tom."

With a look at his cousin, Tom said, "I wasn't sure Ned wanted me to."

Danver waved a hand lazily. "Oh, tell anyone you wish. The notice should appear any day, now."

Kindly, he said to Pomroy, "I am marrying Miss *Sara* Farthingham."

Pomroy looked from the Earl to Tom and said, "So *that's* what you meant!"

"Precisely!" the Earl said, grinning at Tom's discomfort. Then, casually, "Care to accompany the Farthingham ladies and myself to Swinford Abbey, Tom?"

Tom snorted and asserted that nothing could make him desire to spend a week in the company of the spoilt miss who was Sara's cousin. Correctly interpreting this bitterness to be the result of his recent setdown, Danver said soothingly that he knew just how it was. What a pity it was that some females were incapable of appreciating a fellow's excellent qualities. A suspicion crossed Tom's mind that his cousin was roasting him, but Danver's expression was perfectly serious, particularly as the Earl added, "In any case, I quite see that the attractions of a mill must outweigh any female charms. Unless, of course, one is betrothed."

Pomroy looked as though he wished to speak, but was too in awe of his friend's cousin. Not unconscious of the effect he produced on young men just entering the *ton*, Danver chuckled and gave a good-natured wave at the pair as he walked away. At the door of White's, he encountered Sir Tiverton. "Ah, Freddy, there you are again. Good. Meant to ask if you would care to accompany me to Swinford Abbey. I thought I would make up a small house party so that Sara might meet my mother."

From Tiverton's face, it was clear the prospect

held no attraction for him. Still, manfully, he pulled himself together and said carelessly, "Certainly. Happy to oblige. That is, always enjoy visiting the Abbey and like to meet Miss Farthingham again."

Danver laughed and clapped his friend on the shoulder. Coaxingly he said, "Come, come, Freddy! Where is your sense of humour? You've met my mother often enough, and I assure you Sara is no Bath miss. Can't you imagine what it will be like, when they meet?"

Freddy paused, and slowly a grin spread over his face. "By Jove, Ned! You're right. I *should* like to see that. But tell me, why *have* you decided to marry? And why Miss Farthingham?"

Walking jauntily, their voices low enough that passersby could not possibly hear, Danver told him.

9

It was not possible that an announcement of the Earl of Danver's marriage would go unnoticed. As soon as it appeared, friends and acquaintances began calling on the Farthingham ladies, to offer their congratulations and to learn what they could of the matter.

Among Sara's own particular friends, Pamela Winstock was one of the first to call. She and Sara had been close, in school, but had gradually drifted apart after the death of Sara's father, for, naturally, Sara and her mother had withdrawn from society, while Pamela had remained at its centre. She arrived attended by her mother, Jessica Crawford. After greeting Adele and Kitty, Pamela had turned to Sara and said, "Tell me *all* about it, for you must know it was a vast surprise to me, when the notice appeared!"

"Yes," Jessica Crawford said, seating herself by Adele, but addressing Sara, "it was a surprise. Depend upon it, I told Mr. Crawford, it is all a hum. Sara cannot have snared the Earl of Danver."

Kitty would have leapt to her cousin's defense, but a warning look from Adele restrained her. Sara, though she coloured, was able to answer easily, "I am sorry to contradict you, ma'am, but I am indeed betrothed to Lord Danver."

Looking Sara over for a moment, Jessica decided to seek easier prey, and turned her attention to Adele, to see what she could discover. Immediately, Pamela's hand touched Sara's, gently. With genuine concern, she said, "I know this must seem presumptuous of me, Sara, but I must ask if you are quite sure what you are about? One doesn't always realize what marriage may mean. Particularly with a man of ... of Lord Danver's reputation."

Softly Sara replied, "I believe you need have no fear for me, Pamela. I do not go into this marriage expecting Lord Danver to devote all his time to me."

"Yes, but, Sara! Neither did I, with Geoffrey, and yet ..."

As Pamela broke off, in dismay, Sara regarded her friend closely. There had been any number of rumours concerning Mr. Winstock. Pamela's unusual paleness, coupled with the tightness about the mouth, which Sara had never seen before in her friend, caused Sara to wonder if the rumours were true. It was said that even one year's marriage to a devoted wife had not been sufficient to cause Geoffrey Winstock to abandon his bachelor habits, nor to give up his fun among the muslin set. Touched, Sara said impulsively, "Are you so unhappy, then, Pamela?"

She looked down at her gloved hands as she answered, "It would not be so difficult if I had not loved Geoffrey so very much when I married him." There was a pause; then Pamela's chin came up, and she met Sara's eyes squarely. "You mustn't mind me, Sara. It's only that I've become so moped, at times, since I started breeding."

For one incredulous moment, Sara stared at her friend; then she found her voice. "Breeding?"

Now Pamela smiled. "Yes, though I'm only a few months along, and it don't show yet. I hope, so much, that it will be a boy! Geoffrey would like a boy. He said so, just the other night. And, next month, I am to go to our estate in Yorkshire until the baby is born, because Geoffrey is concerned in the centre of London.

"Does Geoffrey go with you?" Sara asked, unable to imagine the dashing Mr. Winstock anywhere save in the center of London.

Some of the brightness left Pamela's face as she said diffidently, "No. He . . . he has business to attend to here. He says he will join me when the baby is due."

I should hope so! Sara thought indignantly. Aloud, she only said, "I am happy for you, Pamela, and hope you will write to me."

Their *tête-à-tête* was broken by Jessica Crawford saying imperiously, "Come along, Pamela, I've some errands to run. Sara, my congratulations. I must say, no one ever looked for you to catch such a prize!"

Upon those words, they left. Adele and Kitty were inclined to be indignant, but Sara was too lost in her own thoughts to care. She could not but feel sorry for Pamela Winstock, nor could she repress the chilling thought that perhaps she would find herself in a similar predicament before the year was out. Why had she agreed to marry Lord Danver? What, after all, did she know of him, save that he was a pleasant companion? Was she a fool to marry a man who felt no *tendre* for her? Sara's only comfort was that John Farthingham, a man whose good sense she trusted, favoured the match. Nevertheless, the doubts she felt were pushed aside, only to recur, and Sara could not banish the spectre of Pamela's unhappy face. It was with trepidation, therefore, that she dressed for Lady Jersey's ball that evening.

Lady Jersey had outdone herself, declaring that this ball was to be the most outstanding one of the season. There were no fewer than three orchestras, two artificial waterfalls, and any quantity of flowers, food, and champagne. Lady Jersey greeted the Farthingham party kindly, and sent them into the ballroom, where Sara was immediately surrounded by friends.

"Is it true?"

"Lady Danver!"

"A countess!"

"Why didn't you tell us?"

On and on, they exclaimed at her, until Sara felt she could bear it no longer. Impossible to answer their questions; impossible to admit the betrothal was not the romantic event it seemed. Where was Lord Danver? Surely, he would rescue her soon?

Lord Danver was, at that moment, on the far side of the ballroom, flanked by his friends Sir Frederick Tiverton and Mr. Anthony Baffington. The three were watching Sara as Baffington said, "Ain't a bad sort, Miss Farthingham. Don't expect a man to do the pretty, when he needs to watch his feet!"

Two pairs of eyes slowly turned to stare at him. Rather in awe, Tiverton asked, "Do you mean to say, Baffy, that *you* have been *dancing?*"

Baffington shrugged uneasily. "Wished to see what sort of woman Ned was taking up with."

Danver stared at Baffington for a moment before saying, "I begin to think I never appreciated the depth of your friendship before, Baffy! Such a sacrifice for you to make!"

"Wasn't!" was the astonishing reply. Then, stoutly, "Enjoyed it. May even do it again."

Still somewhat stunned by his friend's revelation, Danver retorted, "Yes, well, at the moment, I'm the one who ought to be dancing with her. I'm sure you'll excuse me."

Undeterred by the sight of half a dozen females in close conversation, he strode straight to Sara. She could not but feel that he made a handsome sight, with his carefully dishevelled locks and broad, powerful shoulders. Had he but smiled, Sara felt the entire assembly of ladies must have fallen in love with him. But he did not smile. Instead, he bowed, greeted Sara and her friends, and held out a rather peremptory hand, saying, "My dance, I believe, Miss Farthingham."

As he led her onto the floor, Sara could not resist saying, "For one rumoured to be as successful as you, my lord, among the muslin set, you seem to occasionally be remarkably lacking in the social graces!"

He looked down at her rather sternly. "My success, as you call it, is much overrated, I assure you. And, in any event, what do *you* know of such matters?"

Rather taken aback at the strength of his reaction, she said, "Nothing, my lord. I—"

"Edward!" he interrupted her.

"Edward. I only meant to quiz you. Someone said you were fond of such ladies," she could not resist adding, still disturbed by Pamela's visit.

Over her head, Danver said bitingly, "They are not *ladies*. Nor, I assure you, Sara, will you hear such tales after we are married." Then, looking down at her, "Nor do I expect *you* to speak of such things!"

Sara met his eyes steadily, in spite of the anger she saw. "I hear you, my . . . Edward." Then, with a slight smile, "But I thought you did not intend to ride roughshod over me. That sounds, you know, perilously like a command."

His sense of humour touched, Danver smiled, also. "How infamous of me! I beg pardon, but you must know it would not do."

Sara looked away. "I do know it."

The figures of the dance separated them, and when they were next together, Danver appeared to be amused. He looked at Sara with a distinct gleam in his eye as he said, "I'd no notion being engaged could be such an advantage!"

"Oh?" Sara said warily.

Danver chuckled. "Indeed. I seem to have lost whatever quality it was that reduced young ladies to shyness. I've had more conversation directed at me, in this one dance, than I am accustomed to in an evening!"

Sara laughed. "How nice to know I bring you *some* advantages!"

Before Danver could answer, they were again separated by the dance.

It was not to be expected that Danver would dance every dance with Sara. He simply was not that sort of man. Nor was it to be expected that Sara's other suitors would push for her attention, the news of her engagement having become common knowledge. Indeed, Sara might have found herself in the unfortunate position of sitting out, more often than not, had Danver's particular friends not been so obliging. Baffy was somewhat stiff, but Tiverton was very much at his ease and often prompted Sara to laughter, so that Sara thoroughly enjoyed herself, until someone trampled on her gown. She was then obliged to retreat to the rooms set aside for pinning up hems and making similar repairs.

As usual, the rooms were crowded, and though Sara saw no one she knew, she heard her own name being bandied about, freely.

". . . the poor child! Someone ought to warn Miss Farthingham."

"Poor child? I, for one, consider Miss Farthingham

to be odiously sly! You cannot deny that she set her cap for Danver, and the poor man was trapped."

"I still think someone should warn her," the first voice repeated stubbornly.

The second voice laughed maliciously. "It will serve her right! Let her marry him and then see if she enjoys her title. I fancy Lady Danver will have something to say to the matter!"

At this point, the voices were lowered, and Sara could hear no more. She contrived to be bent over her gown, face averted, as the two ladies passed by her. It could not be denied, however, that her confidence was shaken. So, rather soberly, she returned to the ballroom, where she found Lord Danver waiting for her. Seeing her face, he took her hand and said, "What's happened to overset you, Sara?"

"Nothing," she answered, her throat tight.

Danver looked about, discovered two empty chairs, and insisted they seat themselves. Then he spoke, a trifle sternly. "Don't talk flummery! Something has happened, and I wish to know what it is. Have those jealous tabbies been at you?"

This was so near to the truth that Sara flushed. Immediately, Danver's face darkened with anger. "I wish you will not regard it," he said, "for they *are* jealous, you know. And when you are Lady Danver, I hope you may snub them roundly!"

At this, in spite of herself, Sara gave a rather watery chuckle. "And soon I should be an outcast! That uppity Lady Danver who has taken on airs, above herself! That's what they would say of me."

Danver gave a cynical laugh. "I've no doubt they

say such things of *Miss Farthingham*, but once the knot is tied, and they desire your patronage, they will say that Lady Danver's bearing is quite proper, in the wife of an Earl; that she bears herself with suitable dignity! So you see, you shall be quite safe to snub them as you please."

For a brief moment, the pair smiled at each other, in perfect accord. This *tête-à-tête* did not go unnoticed. Even those ladies who had previously expressed skepticism were now forced to own that the notice in the *Morning Post* was not a mistake. Indeed, there was an unbecoming warmth in the way they smiled at each other. It was Mr. Baffington, becoming aware of the glances directed at his friend, who came to Danver's rescue. "May I have this dance, Miss Farthingham?" he demanded boldly.

With some surprise, and a quick glance at Danver, who nodded, Sara agreed. As Baffy led her onto the floor, he said, "Beg you won't take this amiss, but felt it my duty to warn you. All the old tattleboxes watching you and Ned. Knew Ned wouldn't like it. Pair of you looked to be smelling of April and May." He paused, and seeing how quiet Sara was, asked anxiously, "Haven't nabbed the rust, have you? Didn't mean to offend!"

Sara smiled. "No, you're quite out, I'm not offended. Indeed, I'm grateful for your, er, warning."

Baffy nodded. "That's all right, then. Ned would cut up stiff about it, if I was to offend you!"

Ned, however, was thinking, instead, that Sara seemed to be enjoying Baffy's company remarkably well. He could not but be pleased that his choice of bride met with such approval among his friends. Under the circumstances, it was not surprising that neither he nor Sara noticed Kitty's plight.

As might have been expected, the evening began well for Kitty. With the announcement of Sara's engagement, the denial of the rumour concerning Tom and Kitty became credible, and Kitty's court had returned to her side. Including Fitz Hathcart. At the sight of him, bowing in front of her and asking to dance, Kitty turned slightly pale. "N-no, I'm sorry, but I've already promised this dance to . . . to Carsham," she said, naming her nearest admirer.

Carsham's look of surprise was not lost on Hathcart, who bowed and said coldly, "Very well, Miss Farthingham, I hope you may not regret it!"

With those words, he strode off. Carsham would have gone after, to demand what Hathcart meant, but Kitty would not let him. Instead, she insisted they dance. Carsham was only too pleased to oblige. The meaning of Hathcart's threat soon became clear to Kitty as the rumour spread that she had been seen at a Pantheon masquerade. Once more, Kitty began to find that her only partners were rather old, or provincials from the country. At one point, in desperation, she asked George Feathergill, Sara's old friend, to dance. Seeing the look on his face, she added, "Please? I know I ought not to be doing this, but I must know what rumour is being spread about me. There must be a rumour. Why else does everyone fall silent when I approach?"

George Feathergill was indeed appalled by Kitty's forwardness. He also, however, possessed a kind heart, and as they danced, he told her, "Someone's been saying you were at the Pantheon the other night. Don't believe it, of course, but some fellows might."

Kitty had no doubt who was spreading the rumour. Hathcart had good reason to know she had been there, since he was the one who had taken her. Nevertheless, she attempted to answer Feathergill lightly, and succeeded so well that by the end of the dance, he felt that the rumour must be false. Stood to reason that if it wasn't, Miss Farthingham couldn't be so gay. He was not to know that pride, alone, kept Kitty from fleeing the ballroom. But pride would not keep her much longer.

Fortunately, Adele was not oblivious of what was happening. She recognized the danger signs on her young niece's face, and when these had reached alarming proportions, loudly announced that she had the headache and wished to depart. Kitty, when addressed, was curt. "By all means, let us leave. I find this party unbearably insipid."

Adele did not answer, but turned, instead, to one of her admirers. "Mr. Thornby, will you not be so kind as to find my daughter, and inform her I wish to leave?"

"Of course, my dear lady!" Mr. Thornby replied, much flattered.

There was, however, no need for him to carry out this commission, for Lord Danver was approaching, with Sara on his arm. "Ma'am," he said disarmingly, "Sara would have it that you might need her. Will you tell her that she is mistaken, and might remain in my company?"

Distressed, Adele nevertheless insisted, "I'm sorry, my lord, but I am feeling a trifle unwell, and wish to leave."

Instantly, Sara was solicitous. "Of course, Mama! At once!"

Danver was all courtesy. "Permit me to call for your carriage, ma'am."

"Thank you, Lord Danver," Adele said rather faintly.

True to his word, the Earl was soon handing the Farthingham ladies into their carriage. After assuring himself that they were comfortably disposed, he closed the door and told the coachman he might drive them home. Then, although it was not long past midnight, the Earl traced his own steps home.

Meanwhile, despite the best efforts of the carriage maker, the ladies were not finding the ride home at all comfortable. The trouble began when Sara said innocently, "Why did you not ask to leave sooner, Mama? I had no notion you felt ill."

Kitty retorted angrily, "If you had any thought for anyone other than yourself, you would have known!"

Stricken, Sara said, "I'm sorry, Mama!"

Adele, goaded, answered, "No such thing, my love! I only said so because of Kitty."

"Kitty?" Sara said, puzzled.

Rage taking hold, Kitty answered, "You never noticed, did you, that no one wished to dance with me?"

"But I saw you dancing," Sara said, still puzzled.

"With callow boys!" Kitty was scornful. "No one who counts. I can't bear it, Aunt Adele! Even Sara's friend Feathergill avoided me and only danced with me because I asked him to!"

"You asked him to dance with you?" Adele echoed, aghast at this breach of propriety. "What must he have thought?"

"He thought me bold as brass," Kitty answered defiantly, "but it don't signify, for he did dance with me."

Poor Adele fanned herself rapidly, finding no answer to this blunt statement. It was left to Sara to attempt to cope. Soothingly she said, "Perhaps not everyone has heard of my engagement, and they think you bound to Tom?"

Kitty became sullen and silent, and Adele slowly turned to face her niece. "Kitty," she said, in a voice very unlike her own, "I heard some gossip tonight. I denied it, of course, but I wish you will tell me it is untrue. My particular friend, Mrs. Worthing, told me that someone claims to have seen you at a masquerade at the Pantheon. But it cannot be, for I distinctly recall that you had the headache that night and could not accompany us to Almack's. And Charlie brought you late."

Kitty turned a deep red, and Adele waited, "You didn't! And everyone knows you arrived late that night, so there is no use denying the story! How came you to be so reckless as to go, and so heedless as to let yourself be recognized?"

Kitty shrugged scornfully, trying to brazen it out.

"I am not a Puritan, like Sara, and cannot forever be content with dull balls such as Almack's."

Ignoring this, Adele demanded, "Where did you find a domino to wear?"

Again, Kitty was defiant. "It was my mother's. We are of much the same size. And I felt the masquerade could not be so very bad if my mother had gone to one. And she must have, or why should she have a domino?"

Icily aloof, Adele said, "When your mother attended, it was as a young *matron* at a *private* masquerade. She was not a girl barely out of the schoolroom!" Pausing only to determine that Kitty had been sufficiently cowed by this, she went on, "We must hope that the story will be disbelieved as being too improbable. Nevertheless, I must be grateful we are due to leave London tomorrow for Swinford Abbey."

"It was only a harmless prank!" Kitty said defensively.

"Scarcely harmless!" Adele retorted. "These tricks may do very well in the country, though I do not believe it, but they may prove fatal to a young lady's chances here in London. Next I shall hear that you have been refused the entrée to Almack's!"

"I don't care," Kitty said sullenly. "It's a dull, stuffy place."

"Why, so it is," Sara said dryly from her corner of the carriage. "However, it is also, undeniably, the most exclusive of Marriage Marts. If you are indeed denied the entrée there, you may toss over your ambitions for a brilliant alliance."

In the face of Sara's quiet words, Kitty fell silent, for in spite of her brave answers, she felt too keenly the truth of these warnings. The remainder of the journey home was accomplished in grim silence. Nor, once there, could it be said that any of the three ladies sought her bed with any hope of quiet repose.

They would have been even more distressed had they known that, at Lady Jersey's ball, it was also being said that Miss Kitty Farthingham had been maskless at the Pantheon. This was, perhaps, the one detail that might save Kitty. While any number of persons were prepared to believe that Kitty was reckless, capable of coaxing some poor fellow into escorting her to the Pantheon, few could credit that she would do so without a mask. As Mr. Baffington put it, succinctly, when confronted with the story, "Humgudgeon! Never heard of a female going maskless! Fellow who told you must have had windmills in his head! Ten to one, the girl snubbed him and he holds a grudge. Was he bosky? Might only have thought he saw her."

Privately, most of the *ton* agreed with Mr. Baffington. It was the delicious sort of *on-dit*, however, that one simply could not resist telling one's friends. Mothers of daughters with husbands to find were perhaps the most vociferous in spreading the tale.

10

En route to Swinford Abbey, Sara, Kitty, and
Adele rode in the Earl of Danver's own travelling
coach. It was exceedingly well sprung, and not even
Adele could complain of being jolted about. Since it
was such a fine day, Danver and Tiverton chose to
ride alongside. Without meaning to, Sara found her
eyes straying, again and again, to the Earl's commanding figure.

She was a young woman of much common sense,
and it was impossible for Sara not to wonder if she
had mistakenly allowed her heart to overrule her
head. For this, Pamela's warning was, in part, to
blame, as were the words she had overheard the
night before. And partly, it was the example of her
uncle's marriage. John Farthingham had never spoken of his feelings to his niece, but Sara had been

aware that he was often unhappy. Perhaps that was why his approval of this match carried so much weight with her. John Farthingham was not a man to be overawed by worldly success, though he was also not such a fool as to disdain it.

Danver, riding beside the carriage, was also plagued by doubts. Was it fair to Miss Farthingham, to ask her to marry him, at a time when she could not possibly be objective about the matter? Was it fair to himself, to marry a woman who had a *tendre* for another man? His jaw tightened as he thought of his mother. Already he could hear her comments on the subject of Miss Sara Farthingham. Danver did not deceive himself that her pleas, over the years, for him to marry, would reconcile Lady Danver to a daughter-in-law not of her choosing. Particularly a daughter-in-law such as Sara, who could not be depended upon to be conciliatory.

Even Adele Farthingham, seated facing Sara, was not immune to nervousness. She recalled, quite clearly, the first time she had seen Lady Cressilia Danver. It had been at Adele's come-out ball, where Adele had been acknowledged the loveliest girl there. Until the sixth Earl of Danver and his wife arrived. That was, perhaps, the only night of the Season that Adele cried herself to sleep. On the rare, subsequent occasions that they met, Lady Danver had always been polite to her, but Adele could never quite shake the feeling that Cressilia's claws might suddenly appear. And now they were to spend a whole week with the woman!

Kitty, of course, was still feeling shaken by what

had occurred at Lady Jersey's ball. She was well aware that, had this opportunity to leave London not appeared, it would have been necessary to brazen out the gossip. Something Kitty was not at all sure she would have been able to do. But the alternative, hiding, would only have confirmed the rumours. Now, at least, there was a chance that, by the time they returned to London, some other scandal would have replaced the tale of her escapade.

Only Tiverton was capable of enjoying the journey, and he did so, feeling in the best of spirits. Accustomed to his friend's moods, he did not even mind Lord Danver's silence.

At last, the party drew to a halt in front of Swinford Abbey. Danver quickly dismounted, in time to let down the steps and open the carriage door for the ladies. First Adele, then Kitty, and finally Sara emerged. For a moment, as he helped her down, Sara looked up at Lord Danver, anxiously. Instantly his hand pressed hers in reassurance, as he gave her a smile.

Tiverton had also dismounted, and now he flanked Sara's other side as the party approached the steps of Swinford Abbey. Parkins had clearly been on the watch for them, for as Adele reached the first step, the massive oak door swung open and Parkins greeted them impassively, "Welcome, my lord. Ladies. Sir Frederick. Your mother, my lord, is in the drawing room."

"Thank you, Parkins."

Without realizing that she did so, Sara placed her hand on Lord Danver's arm. In the cavernous entryway, she felt sadly dwarfed. Seeing her expression, Danver said, "Courage! She can't eat you, you know."

Sara smiled and shook her head. "It's not your mother I fear. I think it's that I'm in awe of Swinford Abbey. I hadn't expected such . . . such . . ."

"Magnificence?" Danver suggested. "I hope you may learn to like it, for I have always felt at home here."

"I'm sure I shall," Sara said, hoping it was the truth.

Lady Danver and her cousin Henrietta Ramsey were indeed waiting in the drawing room. As a concession to her son, Cressilia had ordered the curtains thrown open and declined a fire in the fireplace. Unaccustomed light, therefore, filled the room and made it seem almost cheerful. The two ladies, themselves, were ranged behind a huge tea tray which had just been sent up.

Cressilia watched the party enter the drawing room, her thoughts rather angry ones. It was not enough that her son had written, *written*, to tell her of his betrothal, but she had barely had time to grasp the news before a note had arrived commanding, *commanding*, her to prepare for visitors! It was a wonder she was not prostrate on her bed with grief. To learn such news in a letter! Lady Danver could only deplore the want of delicacy her only son had shown in announcing to the world his betrothal before he had even brought the girl to meet his mother. If he were capable of such inconsiderate behaviour toward one who ought to command his love and respect, Cressilia could only fear a lapse in judgment, with regard to the young lady herself. Indeed, surely only a certainty, on Edward's part, that Sara Farthingham would displease Lady Danver, could prompt such behaviour. Was Edward so ashamed of her? Or was it Miss Farthingham's doing? Did she seek, even now, before marriage, to come between a son and his devoted mother? Well, Sara Farthingham should find that Cressilia Danver had no compunctions about dealing with such self-serving chits as they ought to be dealt with. If only her health had not forced Lady Danver to return to Swinford Abbey (her debts were conveniently forgotten), she might have been able to protect Edward from all this. Oh, how difficult it was to be a mother!

Having worked herself to a fever pitch of resentment, Lady Danver nevertheless schooled her features to a semblance of graciousness. "Hello, Adele! How long since I've seen you!"

With a sense of being overshadowed, Adele Farthingham replied, "How good to see you, Lady Danver. May I present my daughter, Sara, and my niece, Katherine?"

"Call me Cressy," Lady Danver cooed to Adele, before greeting the two girls. "Ah, Katherine. They call you Kitty, do they not?"

Kitty blushed charmingly, too young to realize that her beauty might arouse jealousy.

Then Lady Danver turned to Sara. Her tone was noticeably cooler as she said, "Hello, my dear. Welcome to Swinford Abbey. It is unfortunate that my health would not permit me to remain in London for the Season. I should like to have made your acquaintance *much sooner*."

Sara met Lady Danver's eyes squarely. Unaware that Tiverton and Danver were watching her intently, some perverse impulse made her say, "I, too, have been looking forward to meeting you and to seeing Edward's home."

Lady Danver stiffened, but then relaxed. If intimidation would not serve to pry loose this hussy, there were other methods. She turned her attention to Danver and his friend. "Hello, Edward. Sir Frederick. I am sure you remember Henrietta, Tiverton." To the Farthingham ladies she explained, "This is my cousin Miss Henrietta Ramsey. She has been kind enough to make her home with me." Then, imperiously, "You may pour the tea, Henrietta. *I* wish to speak with Miss Sara Farthingham. Alone," she added to her son.

The others seated themselves: Danver beside Henny, Tiverton with Kitty and Adele. Thoroughly unruffled, Miss Ramsey began to pour tea, and Danver passed the cups about. The task finally completed, Danver said abruptly, "I think you will like Sara, Henny. Has my mother cut up stiff over the matter?"

Miss Ramsey hesitated. "You must have known she would be distressed, Edward. Immediately she received your letter, she developed Spasms. But I think this house party may answer very well, for you know she will accept the inevitable. Once she has seen that it *is* inevitable. For my part, I'm pleased and wish you happy."

He smiled at her. "Thank you, Henny. I only hope my mother may not try to snub Sara."

Thoughtful, Henrietta stared at Sara, before answering, "Do you know, I cannot imagine you choosing a girl, Edward, who would be intimidated by Cressilia?" Meeting his eyes, she added, "Oh, Edward, I shall be pleased to see you settle down!"

"What? Has my life been so shockingly dissolute?" Danver tried to tease. Seeing it would not do, he turned serious. "I only hope I may not prove a shockingly poor husband."

But Miss Ramsey would not allow this to be possible. "Indeed, I consider Miss Farthingham most fortunate!" she asserted.

He met her eyes, a smile lurking in his own. "Do you? I had the notion *I* was the fortunate one!"

Lady Danver, questioning Sara, was not prepared to agree. Still, his first words were innocuous enough. "Tell me about yourself, Miss Farthingham."

Sara smiled hesitantly, and began to speak. "I was educated at Miss Hensley's School, outside of Bath. Then, three years ago, I was brought out, in London. My father died, directly after my first Season, and we have been living quietly, since. When Kitty turned seventeen, my mother offered to bring her out, for you must know her family lives quietly in the country, and we have been going about again."

"Your interests?" Lady Danver probed. "Music? Sketching? Needlepoint?"

Sara smiled wryly. "I have no talent for sketching or watercolours, and my music is most indifferent. But at least with my needle, I have nothing to blush for, although my best work is practical rather than decorative."

"Are you bookish?" Cressilia demanded.

"I am not above enjoying lively novels," Sara replied, reading her hostess correctly.

Lady Danver nodded, satisfied. Then, unexpectedly, she said, "Edward is my son, and I am sure no one could be more proud of him than I, but are you quite sure you wish to marry him?"

"Ma'am?" Sara said, startled.

Cressilia sighed. "You must know he is inclined to be a trifle thoughtless." She paused to observe the effect of this pronouncement on Sara. Sara merely regarded her steadily, and she went on, "I know this engagement has been contrived very suddenly, and perhaps you should have been given more time to consider? Certainly, Edward should have brought you to see me, first. That's neither here nor there, however, as he did not. I only wish you to know, Miss Farthingham, that if you should feel you have made a mistake, I would support you in your decision to end the betrothal. I am sure I do not wish to press you, but I know what it is to feel impelled into a hasty engagement."

Sara was quiet a moment before saying, somewhat doubtfully, "I thank you for your concern, Lady Danver, but feel it is misplaced."

"Is it?" Cressilia persisted sadly. "Can you say that my son has spoken to you of love?" Seeing that this thrust had gone home, Lady Danver pressed her point. "I know it must seem appealing, the notion of being a countess. But I must tell you that it is not so pleasant as you might imagine. Will you know how to preside over dinners of upwards of fifty guests? Are you prepared to direct a household the size of Swinford Abbey? Have you considered how it must reflect on Edward if you cannot? My dear, I only wish you to think well about the step you are taking."

Seeing Sara fall silent, Lady Danver stood, smoothing her skirts as she did so. "I know you will excuse me, my dear. I must talk with your mother, for we are old friends."

With a smile, she moved to Adele's side, to see what information she might pry out of that lady. Tiverton, who had been talking with Kitty and her aunt, was forced to move, and, seeing that Danver was busy with Miss Ramsey, took the seat beside Sara. Casting about for something to say, he asked, "Well, Miss Farthingham, what do you think of Swinford Abbey? Magnificent, ain't it?"

"Why, yes, it certainly seems so," Sara agreed.

"Not always comfortable, though, particularly in winter," Freddy confided. Seeing that Sara looked unusually serious, he glanced over at their hostess and asked Sara, "Was it very terrible? Lady D ain't known for being kind to Ned's friends, particularly girls. Funny thing, she's always saying it's his duty to marry, but if he looks twice at a girl she ain't picked out for him, Lady D takes snuff and starts snubbing the poor thing, every chance she gets. Mean to say, if she *was* rude, needn't think it's personal. Saw her reduce one chit to tears because Danver waltzed with her, twice, same evening. Any fool could have seen he did it to be kind. Last time I saw Ned waltz, until I saw him with you."

Rather overwhelmed by this confidence, Sara finally managed to cut him short, saying, "Thank you for your warning, Sir Frederick, but I must tell you that Lady Danver was all kindness to me."

"Was she? All the more reason to be careful. I don't trust the woman," Tiverton said frankly.

Unable to cope any longer, Sara desperately turned the subject. "Tell me, sir, is it true that you hold the record for driving from London to Bath?"

No Corinthian could have resisted the opportunity to brag of such a feat, and Tiverton did not even try. That he felt luck had played a large part in his accomplishment, he saw no need to mention. A surprisingly good storyteller, Tiverton even succeeded in making Sara laugh, a feat which escaped none of the other occupants of the drawing room. Kitty immediately pounced on the pair, demanding to know what the jest was. Lady Danver straightened her shoulders and pretended to ignore them. Henrietta, noting the frown on Danver's face, said gently, "She is a very handsome girl, Edward."

"Indeed she is, ma'am."

"And I think a sense of humour an excellent quality, Edward."

"It is, ma'am."

"And she seems very well-bred, Edward, for I

could swear she would much prefer to be talking with us, than with Sir Frederick."

Startled, Danver looked at her, then smiled. "Can you read me that easily, Henny? And is that really your opinion?"

As if in answer, Sara rose and came toward them, carrying her cup. Holding out the cup to Miss Ramsey, Sara said softly but frankly, "I could say I've come for more tea, and indeed I should like some, but actually, I came to join you, if I might."

"Of course, my dear," Henrietta said, making room for Sara beside her on Lady Danver's chaise longue. "May I say you sounded amused, just now?"

Sara smiled engagingly. "Yes, but shall I sound terribly rude if I say that I think that Kitty will enjoy Tiverton's company more than I? And he, hers?"

"Quite right!" Henrietta said, handing Sara a full teacup. "You must know, Edward, that I like Sir Frederick very much, but his understanding cannot be said to be superior. Now, Mr. Baffington is what I suspect you could call a *knowing 'un*."

"I quite agree!" Sara said with feeling.

Amused, Danver said, "Next, I suppose you will call me a slow top?"

Placidly Henrietta answered, "Fustian! You know very well your understanding is superior, Edward, and I have not the slightest intention of pandering to you by saying so!"

"No, you are far more likely to read me a scold!" Danver shot back. "You see, Sara, how I am put upon?"

Sara only laughed and said, "I can see that Miss Ramsey, at least, has not spoilt you dreadfully."

"Oh, no," Henny declared placidly. "I always give Edward my honest opinion. By the bye, now I understand, Edward, why you have been looking so pleased with yourself." Unmanned by this cryptic observation, Sara was relieved when Henny changed the subject by turning to her and saying, "I understand you have a cousin in the military, Miss Farthingham. Tell me, what is his opinion of the situation on the Continent?"

Sometime later, ascending the stairs with Tiverton, Lord Danver said, "Well, Freddy, are you developing a *tendre* for Miss Kitty Farthingham, after all?"

Tiverton laughed self-consciously. "Don't be absurd, Ned, merely because I do the pretty to a chit. Must admit, though, she's a taking thing, ain't she?" Danver dutifully nodded, and Tiverton went on, "Much more sensible than I expected."

This staggering statement left Danver with nothing to say. He could not help wondering, however, what Kitty was up to, this time.

11

Lord Danver was not the only one to note Freddy's interest in Kitty. Or, one perhaps should say, Kitty's pursuit of Sir Frederick Tiverton. Every member of the house party became accustomed to the sight of Kitty appealing to Freddy to answer some question for her. On her best behaviour, Kitty was careful to give Tiverton her most engaging smiles, and to treat him with a shy, admiring deference. Adele could only be pleased at the approval in Tiverton's, whenever they chanced to fall upon Kitty. Particularly in view of the recent events in London. Danver was frankly amused, and it was left to Sara to feel a certain apprehension. Lady Danver was too concerned with her son's betrothal to much care about the other guests, and Miss Ramsey merely observed the situation with her usual good-natured interest.

Actually, the house party went along more pleasantly than anyone might have expected. Adele, pleased at her daughter's engagement and Kitty's apparent success with Sir Frederick Tiverton, even began to feel at ease with Cressilia, who, in spite of her opposition to Sara, rather enjoyed having Adele to gossip with. Particularly as they shared the same taste in novels and card games. Lady Danver, therefore, was condescending to Adele and tolerant of Kitty. Sara, she appeared to take under her wing, instructing her in all the duties of the wife of the Earl of Danver. Edward observed this process, somewhat grimly, but made no effort to interfere. Instead, he occupied himself with the estate. Freddy devoted more and more of his time to Kitty, and wondered why he had not realized how sweet she was in London. Henrietta Ramsey went about her accustomed tasks, showing her usual kindness toward everybody. At one point, she offered to show Sara about the Abbey, deftly turning aside Lady Danver's intention of accompanying them by saying, "Oh, but, Cressy, you *must* think of your health! You know how drafty the northern wing is, and you cannot wish to endure the fatigue of all those stairs?"

Thus appealed to, Cressilia settled her silk shawl closer about her shoulders and said, "Well, I cannot deny there is truth in what you say, Henny, but my duty—"

"Your duty is to Edward," Henrietta answered soothingly, "and how could you fulfill it, if you were to be laid up ill? I can easily show Miss Farthingham about, and she may apply to you, later, Cressy, for all the family history of the rooms."

Lady Danver capitulated, not altogether loath to spend the time exchanging *on-dits* with Adele. Danver had long since left them, in order to look over his accounts, and Kitty and Tiverton had chosen to take a turn about the gardens.

As promised, the northern wing was quite drafty, and Henrietta confided, "*We* rarely use it these days. I understand there was a time when Swinford Abbey was always full of house guests, and one can only pity those guests forced to use this wing. I cannot but feel that mosaic tile was not the most felicious choice for bedroom floors, but the present Earl's grandfather visited Italy in his youth, and conceived a passion for it. Fortunately, the wife of the fifth Earl contrived to restrict his improvements to this wing. I understand she was a most redoubtable lady."

If the northern wing appeared Italian, the central portion of the house was quite traditional. Heavy tapestries hung on some of the walls, and Belgian carpets covered the floors. Furnishings were elegant but entirely British in origin. The rooms themselves were large and relatively comfortable, and one's greatest cavil was likely to be that there was an extraordinary number of doors, as apartments opened into one another. In addition, this portion of the Abbey was not at the same level as the northern or southern wings, and one was forced to go up or down half a flight of stairs to enter either wing.

The southern wing of the Abbey was given over to
galleries, drawing rooms, the library, and a vast ballroom. It was decorated almost entirely in the French
mode, save for the library that Edward had so eccen-
trically insisted upon decorating himself. At the far
end of this wing, added onto the building, the bailiff, Mr. Bowen, had a small set of apartments. The
sixth Earl of Danver, in hiring the youngest son of a
clergyman, had felt impelled to provide the fellow
with something more appropriate than the usual
tenant cottage. So he had had these apartments built
and placed them at Mr. Bowen's disposal. They
could be reached only by going outside.

Sara found the portrait gallery fascinating. The
first Earl of Danver was a grim-faced fellow who
looked as though he gave a damn about no one save
himself. His lady looked like a shy, timid creature,
and Sara could not help pitying her. The next three
earls shared the same determined features, softened
by the self-assurance that comes with an hereditary
title. Their wives were the embodiment of good
breeding and serious demeanour, although Miss
Ramsey did murmur something about there being
no portrait of the third Earl's first wife, who had
been rather unusual. The portraits of the sixth Earl
of Danver and his wife, Cressilia, were quite different. The couple looked very young and very gay, almost defiantly so. Then they reached Edward's
portrait. He stared out at them, his features haughty
and stern. Compared to his parents, he must have
seemed a changeling, had he not had the classic Fambrough features. Sara spent some time staring at the

portrait. Standing quietly beside her, Henrietta said, "Edward has not had an altogether happy life. His parents have always felt him too serious and, at the same time, too heedless. Lady Danver is most concerned about him, and I hope you will not be offended if her zeal carries her to extremes, at times." After a moment, she added, "I feel sure that you and Edward will deal well together. In time, Cressilia will come to realize that, also."

Once more, Sara felt at a loss and could only ask to see the next room. She felt incapable of entering into a discussion of her relationship with Lord Danver, when she was so uncertain of her own mind.

They were still in the French wing when they encountered Mr. Bowen. He was coming from the library, and paused as soon as he saw the two ladies. Intrigued, Sara noted the smile on Miss Ramsey's face and the softening of Mr. Bowen's expression. "Good day, Mr. Bowen," Henrietta said, her voice a trifle tremulous. "May I present Miss Sara Farthingham, his lordship's fiancée?"

Mr. Bowen bowed. "Hello, Miss Farthingham. May I wish you happy?"

Sara decided that she liked his open, friendly expression and impulsively held out her hand as she said, "Thank you, Mr. Bowen. How nice to meet you."

He smiled at her, then turned to Henrietta. "Perhaps I might speak with you later, Miss Ramsey?"

Her curiosity whetted, Sara said, "If you would like to talk now, I'm sure I can find my way back alone."

Her eyes twinkling, Henrietta said very primly, "I ought not to take advantage of your very generous offer, Sara, but I think I shall."

Smiling as fantasies of romance ran through her head, Sara left them. She had not gone far when she encountered Lord Danver. His hand was on the library door and he was frowning, slightly, in spite of the fact that he must have been aware Sara looked quite charming. "Hello, Sara. Were you looking for me?" he asked.

Sara shook her head. "At the risk of seeming rude, I must say that I was not. Henny was showing me about the Abbey."

"Where is she, then?" he asked, puzzled.

Carefully keeping her countenance serious, Sara replied airily, "Oh, we encountered Mr. Bowen, and he wished to consult her on some small matter."

To her surprise, Danver began to chuckle. "Did he? Yes, I can see that you might have been *de trop*." Smiling down at Sara, Danver explained, a twinkle in his eyes, "I suspect Mr. Bowen wished to propose to Henny."

Sara was startled into saying, "You don't mind?"

Immediately, Sara coloured deeply, but Danver was only amused. Waving her into the library, and indicating a chair near one of the windows, he said, "Why should I? Mr. Bowen is of a respectable family. My father would never have trusted a bailiff who was not a gentleman. And, in any case, my primary concern must be Henrietta's happiness. No, my mother is the one who will dislike the match. Do you?"

This last question was spoken bluntly, and Sara met Danver's eyes squarely. She answered equally bluntly, "How should I? It is none of my affair. And, in any case, I like Miss Ramsey and would like to see her happy." Sara paused and smiled. "I've a notion that Mr. Bowen will see that she is." Sara paused again, then asked hesitantly, "If your mother opposes the match, won't it be awkward for them, living here, with her?"

"No. Because once *we* are married, my mother will remove to the Dower House," he explained frankly. "I would prefer, however, that you not mention this matter to anyone. If my mother should hear of it too soon, she might contrive to make Henny rather unhappy."

"I shan't tell anyone," Sara assured him. Then, "You're very fond of Miss Ramsey, aren't you?"

"Henny?" The Earl had half-turned away, but Sara could see his face clearly. "Yes, I am. She's a sensible woman who has been kind to me, and I wouldn't see her hurt, for anything. She came to live with us, with my mother, when my father was dying, and she is the only person I've ever been able to talk to about him. Perhaps because she has known so much grief herself, she understood mine." After a moment, Danver shook his head, as if to clear it, and said briskly, "Well, how do you like my library?"

Sara looked it over, carefully, before saying, "It's beautiful. Indeed, I hope you don't mind my saying so, but I like it better than any of the other rooms I've seen here at Swinford Abbey."

"I'm relieved to hear you say so," Danver retorted

wryly. "As my wife, you must have the right to decorate the rooms as you wish, but I am relieved to know that your taste accords with mine."

The reminder, spoken aloud, brought Sara to her feet, anxious to avoid his eyes. Restlessly she traced her fingers along a row of books, as Danver watched, his face impassive. For several minutes he tolerated her questions about his books, then said, abruptly, "Would you care to see the maze? It's at its best, this time of year."

Clearly, the maze was a source of pride at Swinford Abbey. The shrubbery stood eight feet high and was well pruned. Drawing Sara's hand through his arm, Danver walked slowly, as though he could think of nothing better to do than to stroll about with Sara. As they walked, Danver asked Sara for her impressions of Swinford Abbey. She answered frankly, "There is much to admire. One couldn't call it a comfortable house, precisely, but one has the feeling that someone cared very much about each part of it. Moreover, the grounds and prospect are such as must please, and I would guess that the gardens are particularly lovely in the summer."

Danver nodded, as though satisfied, and paused. They had, by this time, reached the entry to the maze, and he explained, "This is the second maze which has stood on this spot. The first one was supported by wooden trellis and was burnt to the ground by the wife of the third Earl of Danver. Supposedly, she was running away with her lover, and wanted the Earl to know, clearly, how she felt."

As they entered the maze, Sara said, appalled,

"What a horrid thing to do! Was there any justification for it? Was the third Earl such an ogre?"

Danver looked at Sara, his expression unreadable. "No one knows. He appears handsome enough in the portrait, but I gather he was twice her age and preferred to keep her here, away from Society and young men her own age. Does that qualify him as an ogre?"

"She should not have married him, if he was twice her age," Sara said bluntly. "Not unless she loved him, and in that case, she would scarcely have run off with another man. Is it certain she did so?"

"Quite certain. She was brazen about the whole business, going about openly with the fellow in Paris. The third Earl remarried, after her death, and at the age of eighty, fathered the fourth Earl of Danver." Edward paused, then added softly, "I would guess that neither bride had much choice in her marriage. In view of that, I suppose it is not surprising that the first one ran away."

"No, not surprising at all," Sara agreed thoughtfully. "I, too, would run away, if I felt a marriage unbearable." Then, realizing what she had said, Sara blushed deeply.

Danver looked at her steadily, his eyes very serious. They had reached, by now, the centre of the maze, and he indicated that Sara should sit on the marble bench. When she had done so, he said, still standing, "Perhaps it's time we talked frankly about our betrothal, Sara. Do you wish out of it?"

She hesitated, then asked, "Do you?"

"I'm not the one who has just been talking about running away," he answered sternly.

Sara coloured again. "Th-that has nothing to do with us! I was talking about the third Earl, not you."

Danver would have probed further had they not heard a voice calling urgently, "Sara! Sara!"

Immediately, Sara was on her feet. "Kitty, I'm coming!" Then, to Edward, "I must go see what Kitty is upset about."

Danver cursed, under his breath, stood aside for her to pass, then followed, knowing she would need his help in finding her way out of the maze. Kitty was waiting for them when they emerged, and even to Danver it was obvious she was very upset. "What's wrong?" he asked at once.

Kitty hesitated only briefly, decided by the unexpected concern evident in his voice. Sara and Danver might be older, and, from Kitty's point of view, rather staid; nevertheless, she felt they could be counted upon for help. Sara, at least, had always come to her rescue in the past. Taking a deep gulp, Kitty held out a letter to Sara. "It's from Ellen Worthing," she explained. "She writes to tell me that all of London is talking about me!"

"An exaggeration," Sara countered, as she took the letter from Kitty's outstretched hand.

"No, I think not," Kitty answered thoughtfully. Then she stopped, looking warily at Danver.

"That silly story about the Pantheon, I suppose?" Danver suggested helpfully.

"It's not a silly story!" she retorted indignantly. "I *was* there! And Fitz Hathcart—he was the man who

took me, Sara—is going about telling everyone. And
. . . and the man who tore my mask must have
recognized me somewhere, or else someone saw me
with it torn, and they . . . he must also be talking,
for Ellen says the gossip is that I went maskless! But
I didn't! I must consider myself ruined!"

Sara, after hearing Charles's report of how he had
found Kitty, had no trouble following her cousin's
words. "Nonsense!" she retorted briskly. "By the
time we return to London, some other scandal will
be on everyone's tongue. So long as you are careful,
and do nothing indiscreet, you will be forgiven this
escapade."

"*Forgiven*?" Kitty demanded hotly. "Why must I
be forgiven anything? What I did was nothing so
very terrible! It's not my fault if the *ton* surrounds
me with impossible rules that I cannot and will not
obey!"

"Then you are a fool!" Danver said harshly.

Giving him a look of pure hatred, Kitty said, "I
should have guessed you wouldn't understand!"

Then, gathering her skirts with one hand, the
other covering her mouth, Kitty ran across the long
lawn toward the Abbey. "Kitty!" Sara called after
her, in sympathetic protest.

"Foolish girl!" Danver repeated softly.

To herself, Sara could only agree. She felt compelled, however, to defend Kitty. Impulsively she
said, "You cannot know what it is for a spirited girl
like Kitty to be obliged to follow the endless rules
and regulations that hem in our lives. Indeed, I cannot be surprised that Kitty feels she cannot bear it!"

"And you? Do you feel the same?" Danver demanded.

Defiantly Sara retorted, "At times!"

His mouth suddenly quirked into an engaging smile as he said, "The wives of the Earls of Danver have generally been noted for their devotion to propriety."

Unfortunately, Sara didn't see the smile, and it was wiped away by her next words. Stiffly she said, "I know it, and if I had not, your mother has taken pains to assure that I understand. Indeed, in these past few days I have begun to wonder how you could have chosen to propose to me. I know very well that I have neither the ancestry nor the wealth nor the submissive nature that might have rendered me acceptable to your family."

Anyone intimately acquainted with the Earl would have instantly recognized the signs of anger: the set face, the hands clasped tightly behind his back, the darkened colour of the eyes that searched Sara's face. His voice was deadly calm as he said, "Do I understand, Miss Farthingham, that you begin to feel our betrothal was an error?"

"Yes. No. How can I say?" Sara answered, distraught, yet feeling she must be frank. "Your mother—"

"We will leave my mother's opinion out of this discussion!" Danver retorted bitingly. Too far gone in his rage to consider his words, he added, "I will thank you to remember, ma'am, that we *are* engaged, and I will not tolerate the betrothal being broken!"

"And I take leave to tell *you*, Lord Danver, that,

should I decide the betrothal was a mistake, I would run away, even elope with another man, sooner than marry you!" she answered heatedly. Then, gathering *her* skirts, she followed Kitty's example and fled to the house.

Danver could only watch her, cursing both her temper and his. Then he turned and headed slowly for his library. En route, however, he encountered Freddy, who immediately said, "I say, Ned! What's wrong?" Then hastily he added, "Needn't tell me, if you don't wish to."

"I don't!" Danver retorted bluntly. "What I *do* wish to do is go over to the Blue Fox and have dinner there. Join me, Freddy?"

"What about the ladies?" Tiverton asked, a trifle uneasy. "Don't like to offend them."

Danver regarded his friend oddly before saying, "If you mean Sara, I assure you she won't mind."

Beginning to feel distinctly alarmed, Freddy agreed to the scheme with alacrity. It had occurred to him that if something were indeed wrong, it would be far more comfortable to be away from the Abbey. Aloud he said, "Right, Ned! As I recall, they've a nice burgundy. Or is it the sherry?"

"Neither! It's the brandy you're thinking of!" Danver retorted, amused in spite of himself. "Come along, we'll ride over."

The two men escaped a far more unpleasant evening than either could have guessed. Lady Danver, having seen both Kitty and Sara running, delivered a homily over the first course at dinner. "In *my* day, I am thankful to say, young ladies were given rather less freedom. Impossible to imagine any of us, Henny, Adele, *running* about like country farmgirls! *We* were brought up to think of our positions, for with the privileges of being one of the *ton* come certain responsibilities. I shudder to think what Edward must feel, were he to see his future wife so far forgetting herself!"

Too angry to consider her words, Sara replied evenly, "You are free to ask him, ma'am, for he did see me."

Adele and Cressilia regarded Sara with horror, and even Henrietta seemed perturbed. Her voice quivering with indignation, Lady Danver said, "I see. This is, I presume, the reason we do not have my son with us this evening?"

Lowering her head slightly, Sara said, "I don't know, ma'am. In any event, it must be a matter between Lord Danver and myself."

Lady Danver's eyes narrowed before she turned to Adele. Silkily she said, "And you, Adele? Do you agree with your daughter and niece that such behaviour is acceptable?"

Feeling wretched, Adele tried to answer. She could not but resent Sara and Kitty for placing her in this position; nevertheless, she must defend them. "Surely, in the country, where no one can see—"

"*No one can see?*" Cressilia echoed indignantly. "I should not have said that I was quite No One, Adele!"

"Oh, of course not!" Adele protested hastily. "I only meant no one other than . . . than . . ."

"Family?" Henrietta supplied calmly. "For you

must agree, Cressy, that with Edward's betrothal, the Farthinghams *are* almost family."

Lady Danver glared at her companion a moment before retorting spitefully, "If she has not given him so great a disgust of her that he breaks the engagement!"

Once more, Henrietta's voice answered calmly, "Oh, I think not, Cressy. Recollect that, as your son, he could scarcely be so ill-bred."

Not unnaturally, this silenced Lady Danver, for whatever her true feelings, she could not openly refute such a statement. With difficulty, the Farthingham ladies restrained themselves from cheering Miss Ramsey.

It was a most unpleasant evening.

Lord Danver was finding his own evening rather trying. The landlord of the Blue Fox had indeed set an excellent dinner before them, in his private parlour, and there was the promise of his best brandy after. The problem was Tiverton. Freddy was, in general, a good fellow and properly reserved. Wine, however, occasionally loosened his tongue, and it was quickly borne in upon Lord Danver that this was going to be one of those occasions. It was somewhere over the second course that Tiverton began to speak his mind. "Nice girl, Miss Farthingham. Both Miss Farthinghams," he added judiciously. "Never thought to see you a tenant-for-life, Ned. At least, not so soon. Agree with Baffy, though. Think it might answer very well. Though what the devil *he* meant by that, don't know. Miss Sara a most amiable

choice for you. Sorry to see any trouble come between you. Mean to say, if there should be trouble,
happy to offer my services to mediate."

"So you approve of Sara, do you?" Danver asked,
torn between anger and amusement.

Freddy pondered the question for several moments before replying, "Yes, I do. Too knowing, by
half, for me, but just the girl for you, Ned. Thought
before, maybe the reason none of the chits you've
met has caught your fancy is they bored you. Not a
man to be satisfied with a pretty face, Ned. Well,
stands to reason, *you* need someone you can talk
with. Me, I wouldn't know what to say to Miss Sara,
half the time. But can't help seeing that you do. Not
likely to be bored."

"No," Danver conceded, with a half-bitter laugh,
"I'm not likely to be bored with Sara."

"There you are, then!" Freddy said triumphantly.
"Hope you'll patch up your quarrel."

Danver regarded his friend with exasperation. To
anyone else, he would have denied that there had
been any quarrel. Danver knew, however, that in
Freddy's present state, such a denial would have no
effect and might even encourage the fellow to pursue the matter further.

Dinner was followed by the brandy, which had a
predictable effect on Tiverton. Danver gave the
landlord precise instructions for the morning, and
then helped him carry Freddy upstairs to the best
bedchamber. Before he left, Danver paid the shot.

The ride back to Swinford Abbey helped to clear
Danver's head, and he was feeling considerably bet-

ter as he entered, stripping off his riding gloves. To his astonishment, he found his mother waiting for him. Instantly she began to regale him with her account of the dinner discussion. She ended by saying, "As for what Society will say of your marriage, Edward, I shudder to think! But so I knew it must be when I found my health would not permit me to stay in London, at your side. I should never have forsaken my duty."

"Mother"—Danver's voice held an unmistakable menace—"if we are to talk of *my* nuptials, perhaps we had best talk of *your* removal to the Dower House." He paused, and seeing that he had silenced her, said quietly but firmly, "Good night, Mother."

12

It was a much diminished group that gathered at the breakfast table the next morning. Both Adele and Cressilia chose to keep to their rooms, and Tiverton, of course, slept on, quite peacefully, at the Blue Fox. Of those who did gather—Danver, Miss Ramsey, Kitty, and Sara—three were ill-at-ease. Impossible for Kitty and Sara not to feel apprehensive about encountering Lady Danver. Even more uncertain, for Sara, was the question of how to face the Earl. Nor would it have reassured her to know that he was out of temper. It would have been difficult enough, Danver felt, to face Sara after the previous day's fight, had that been all. But it was not. There was also the effect of his mother's outspoken anger at Sara to be dealt with.

Miss Ramsey, alone, was calm. As usual, she was

the first to reach the breakfast room, and the others found her placidly prepared to pour out tea and coffee. When everyone had appeared, she quietly announced, "Poor Cressy, Lady Danver, passed a rather indifferent night, I'm afraid, and I expect she will keep to her room most of the day."

Kitty brightened perceptibly at this, and Sara could not but feel relief. All Sara said, however, was, "My mother also passed an indifferent night and will not be joining us."

Danver did not fail to note the tension and the way it eased at Henrietta's words, or to guess at the reason for it. This was, he felt, an intolerable situation for them all. Frustration made him say, more abruptly than he intended, "Sara, I must ride out to see some of my tenants today, and it's rather urgent. When I return, this evening, however, I should like to speak with you."

Hearing the anger in Danver's voice, Sara assumed it was directed at her. Stiffly she replied, "I am at your disposal, whenever you wish."

Oblivious of the undercurrents between her cousin and the Earl, Kitty broke in to ask, with an air of innocence, "Lord Danver, will Sir Frederick be riding out with you?"

He answered curtly, "I shall be much surprised if Tiverton returns to the Abbey by the time I must leave. When I left him at the Blue Fox last night, he was being put to bed in the best bedchamber. And I expect he'll have the devil of a head this morning."

Kitty's reply was merely a thoughtful "Oh."

Amused, Danver said, "I most mistrust you, Miss

Farthingham, when you speak so innocently. I can only hope that while I am gone, you can manage to avoid any further scandal."

"I hardly think Kitty could find a way to create a scandal here, on your estate," Sara retorted coolly.

"No? Perhaps I credit her with greater imagination than you do," Danver answered impatiently. "Recollect that I know of no female who has ever ruined herself in so short a time as Kitty."

"You shan't say I'm ruined, you shan't!" Kitty said, white with fury.

"No?" was the soft reply.

"I think you go too far!" Sara said icily. "Imprudent she may have been, but that is all I will allow."

Even Henny said, in her quiet voice, "Don't you think that perhaps you exaggerate, Edward?"

Danver regarded them ironically for a moment, then inclined his head, saying, "I bow to your collective superior judgment." Setting down his cup, he added, "Now, you must excuse me. I have work to do!"

When he was gone, Kitty said, her bosom heaving, "How dare he say such things about me?"

Sara tried to answer gently, "Well, you must seem to him a trifle volatile, you know, Kitty."

Indignantly Kitty turned on her cousin. "I see how it is—even you abandon me! I never thought *you* could be so heartless!"

Then she, too, was gone. Sara, watching her cousin's angry exit, was startled to hear Henrietta say quietly, "I think I shall ask the staff to send luncheon trays to everyone's room today. It will be much the best solution, don't you think?"

Their eyes met, with perfect understanding, and Sara said softly, "Yes, I quite agree."

Miss Ramsey smiled and added, "I have always found long walks to be beneficial for sorting out one's thoughts." In spite of herself, Sara smiled. Satisfied, Henrietta rose to her feet, saying, "I know you will excuse me, my dear. I must go see if Cressy needs me."

Sara nodded. She could not but feel a strong wave of affection for this calm, sensible woman who was such a contrast to Lady Danver. Tiverton had been quite right when he called her a *prime 'un!* Recollecting his words, Sara also found herself wondering, half-amused, whether the case with Tiverton was as bad as Danver had predicted.

It was, in fact, worse.

The clock struck eleven before Freddy managed to pull himself upright. His stomach and head both protested, and he would have retreated to the bed had the landlord not knocked just then. "Come in!" Tiverton snarled, expecting his friend Danver. Seeing who it was, he demanded, "What do you want? I wish you will go away!"

"Begging your pardon, sir," the landlord answered, "his lordship said as how you might be wanting something for your head. It's my own recipe, and most efficacious."

Freddy's impulse was to pour the proffered noxious mixture over the landlord's head. He was desperate enough, however, to drink it instead. Two hours, and a neat luncheon, later, Tiverton was riding toward Swinford Abbey, feeling considerably better, though still not his usual self.

Leaving his horse at the stable, Freddy rather reluctantly headed for the house. His path took him through the gardens, where, to his surprise, he found Miss Katherine Farthingham crying. Never an overly perceptive fellow, Freddy was even less so after an evening spent under the hatches. "Here! I say, Miss Farthingham! What's wrong?" he asked, dismayed.

Looking up, as if seeing Sir Frederick Tiverton for the first time, Kitty hastily tried to smile. "N-n-nothing," she answered bravely.

Tiverton stared at her, frowning. "Nothing! Don't believe it. Wouldn't be crying if it were nothing. Stands to reason. Don't wish to tell me, that's what it is! Needn't, then."

Kitty's eyes flew up to his and, rather breathlessly, she said, "Oh, but I do wish to tell you! Only . . . only, there is nothing anyone can do to help, and I don't wish to burden you with my problems." Seeing that Freddy was about to agree with her, she went on quickly, "I don't know why it should be that I wish to confide in you, except, perhaps, that I can see you would understand so well. One quite feels *you* would know what to do."

Sir Frederick, who had been silently congratulating himself on escaping the girl's teary confidence, was startled. No one had ever indicated, before, that they considered his advice desirable. Kitty's words had their effect, and he found himself saying, "There, there, Miss Farthingham. Ten to one, the problem is not as difficult as it seems." Sitting down beside her, he invited, "Come, tell me about it, and we will put our heads together and contrive *something.*"

Her eyes hidden by her long, lowered lashes, Kitty said softly, "It's my brother Charles. I've had a note from the landlord of the Duck and Crown. My . . . my brother was coming to see me, and his curricle overturned and he is lying injured at that inn. I *must* go and nurse Charlie, but I haven't the faintest notion how to get there."

"Ned'll send you and your aunt in his carriage," Tiverton replied promptly.

"But my aunt mustn't know!" Kitty said instantly. "You see, the doctor said she wasn't to have any . . . any shocking news."

"Lady Farthingham? Seems in fine fettle to me," Tiverton said with a frown.

"Generally she is," Kitty assured him. "It is only on this one thing we must be careful. Though," she added judiciously, "in any event, Aunt Adele would not wish anyone to worry about her. Sara says that her mother is merely indisposed this morning, but you can understand that I particularly do not wish to . . . to distress her today?"

She turned her eyes up to him appealingly, and Freddy said, "Yes, of course. Your sentiments do you credit. I have it! Go with Sara! Ned would be happy to lend you his carriage."

Again Kitty lowered her eyes. "But . . . but I do not wish to take Sara away from her mother, in case . . ." She paused, took a deep breath, and went on, "Lord Danver rode out early, saying he won't be back before nightfall. So you see, there is no solution."

His head still a bit muddled, it took some time for Freddy to consider the matter. Finally, however, he said, "I'll take you. Only thing to do. Is it far?"

Her eyes wide, Kitty said, "Oh, no, I don't wish to put you out, Sir Frederick! You've been so kind to me, and I won't trespass on your good nature."

"Nonsense!" he retorted briskly, his chest swelling slightly. "Wish to do it. Is it far?"

"Not above forty miles," Kitty assured him. "Oh, Sir Frederick, I think you're wonderful!"

"There, there," he said, as she gazed at him in admiration. "You go get ready, and I'll order a carriage brought round front."

She smiled a dazzling smile as she said, "I shall be ready in a trice. Naturally, I must leave a note for Sara, but I shan't tell anyone else, for fear that Aunt Adele will hear of it. I shall simply say we are going for a drive, and when you return, this evening, you can explain."

This, however, was too much for Tiverton, and he protested, "No, here, must tell someone else!"

Kitty considered a moment, then said brightly, "Very well. I'll tell Miss Ramsey."

Tiverton gave a sigh of relief. "Good notion. She'll know what to say to 'em."

Kitty nodded and was gone. Tiverton wandered back to the stables, feeling rather pleased with himself. He would not have been so pleased could he have known what Kitty was about. She not only did not speak to Henrietta Ramsey, but, encountering Sara, on her way upstairs, Kitty told her cousin she intended to rest in her room for the afternoon. Once upstairs, Kitty quickly thrust a change of raiment in one of her bandboxes, as well as a few other necessities. The note for Sara was, oddly enough, already written, and it only needed pinning to her pillow before Kitty was ready to depart. Carefully creeping downstairs, Kitty slipped out the front door unseen. Tiverton, waiting, gaped at the sight of the bandbox. Looking at him sweetly, Kitty explained in a low voice, "Oh, these are a few things that might help me to nurse Charlie!"

Tiverton nodded, then demanded, "Where's your abigail?"

A look that might have been exasperation crossed her face and was quickly gone. Breathlessly she said, "Oh, but Sara and I share Betsy, and besides . . . besides, my aunt depends on her, when she is not feeling quite the thing. If it looks as though I am to stay long with Charlie, she can join me, bringing my things."

Tiverton nodded. It sounded reasonable to him. Satisfied, he handed her into the carriage. Ascertaining from Kitty that the Duck and Crown was on the post road, some forty miles to the east, Tiverton passed this information on to the coachman. Then they were off. Nor did Kitty cavil that Tiverton had chosen to take Danver's travelling coach, not the most rapid of vehicles. By the time the alarm was raised, it would be too late. Sir Frederick would have been already compromised, trust her for that!

Roughly an hour later, unaware of the accident which was supposed to have befallen him, Major Charles Farthingham bowled up the drive in a post-chaise and four. It pulled up in front of Swinford Abbey, and Farthingham stepped out, telling the postboy, "Drive 'em around to the stables. I don't know how long I shall be."

A few minutes later, an impassive Parkins was announcing Major Charles Farthingham to Miss Sara Farthingham. Sara was immediately on her feet and holding out her hands to Charles under Parkins' disapproving gaze. Parkins was devoted to the Earl and was well aware that Miss Sara had never greeted his lordship with such unbecoming warmth. Impeccably trained, however, Parkins regretfully withdrew, just as Sara was demanding, "Charles! What are you doing here?"

"Sara, how are you? I've come to say good-bye. I'm on my way to the Continent, you see."

"So soon?" He nodded, and Sara sighed. "Well, then, I'd best go find Kitty and Mama so that you can say good-bye to them, as well."

She would have gone, but Charles detained her by holding on to her hand. "In a moment, Sara. First I want to talk with you about Lord Danver. My father told me what happened, and I must know if this is what you really wish for."

Sara looked down, unable to meet his eyes. Attempting to turn the subject, she said quickly, "Of course! But I have not yet had the chance to tell you how pleased I was to hear that your father has given his consent to your betrothal to Lisette."

Charles gave her a warm smile. "It is wonderful news, isn't it? And I promise you, you will adore Lisette! Which is why," he added, becoming stern again, "I am so concerned for you. I know what love can be, and cannot believe you will truly be content with so much less."

"Surely that is my affair?" Sara retorted, a hint of steel in her voice.

For a moment, Major Farthingham looked as though he wished to shake his cousin. Finally he said, "So it is. And if you insist you are satisfied, then there is no more to be said but to wish you happy. But it still seems dashed irregular to me!" he ended bluntly.

Sara smiled, in spite of herself. "I know," she said gently. "But please believe I do not feel myself forced into anything."

"Very well," Charles said quietly. "And now perhaps you had better go find Kitty and Aunt Adele. I haven't much time to spare here."

"I'll be back in a moment!" Sara promised.

Sara was gone considerably longer than a moment, however, and when she returned, she was alone and carried a heavy cloak over her arm.

"What the devil?" Charles exclaimed, at the sight of her. Wordlessly, Sara handed him the note she held.

My dearest Cousin Sara,

I only hope that when you discover what I have done, you will Understand and Forgive me. I have Run Off with Sir Frederick Tiverton. He has no notion, of course, of what I am about, and believes himself to be driving me to meet my brother Charles. (I have told him Charles was injured.) It is of No Use to pursue us. Somehow I will keep him by my side, tonight, and prevent either of us from returning to Swinford Abbey. Tiverton is a gentleman and I have no doubt will do the Proper Thing.

I shrink from such a step, but it has become clear to me that I am already ruined and have no other way to Come About. Sir Frederick has been kind to me, and I believe he will make an amiable husband, once he becomes accustomed to the notion.

Forgive me, Sara, and try to allay the fears of anyone who may be concerned about me. I need not tell you, however, that these details are intended for your eyes only. I remain your loving cousin,

Kitty

Charles looked up from the note, his face pale. "Is my sister mad?" he demanded.

"I begin to wonder!" Sara replied bitterly, her face as pale as his. "We must, of course, go after them. Though how we may find them, I haven't the faintest notion."

Charles thought rapidly. "I'll go round to the stables and order my post-chaise brought up. Perhaps someone there will have heard something that may help us."

Sara nodded. Together they went to the entry hall

so that Charles could retrieve his hat, cape, and gloves. Parkins surrendered them silently, a slight frown on his face at the sight of Sara's cloak. Then he retreated. He was not yet out of earshot, however, when he heard the Major say, "Do *you* wish to leave a note for anyone? Your mother, Sara? Lord Danver?"

Parkins was so astonished that he forgot himself and shamelessly eavesdropped as Miss Farthingham replied, "No. I've no wish to upset my mother. As for Danver, I . . . I should prefer he knew nothing about it. He is angry enough, already, and I've no wish to have him after us, as I think he would be, if he knew the truth. No, we must trust that everyone merely concludes that we have gone for a drive."

Charles was not altogether convinced, but he only said, "Very well. As you wish. I shall go get the carriage and meet you in front in a few minutes. Which way is shortest to the stables?"

Parkins hastily withdrew, wishing his lordship were at the Abbey. Impossible to approach her ladyship, particularly when she was indisposed. Equally impossible to confide in one of the guests or one of the other servants. Nor could Parkins see any way for *him* to prevent Miss Sara from eloping with this gentleman, for elopement it plainly was, even if the fellow had said he was her cousin. Cousins had been known to marry before!

Unaware that Parkins had overheard them, Sara was nonetheless anxious to be gone. She had no wish to encounter any member of the household who might ask awkward questions. With relief, she started down the steps as the post-chaise and four came into sight, only to halt as she saw the figure of Miss Henrietta Ramsey coming across the lawn toward the Abbey. The chaise drew up and the door was flung open as Charles emerged to hand his cousin into the carriage. Before he could do so, Henrietta reached them. Puzzled but calm, the lady said, "Hello, Sara."

Her voice trembling only slightly, Sara said, "Miss Ramsey, may I present my cousin Major Charles Farthingham? Charles, this is Miss Henrietta Ramsey."

The pair exchanged conventional greetings, and Charles then said, with a confiding air, "I've seen too little of my cousin, this visit to London, and I want to take her for one last drive before I leave for the Continent."

Henrietta smiled and nodded, too well-bred to voice her puzzlement. All she said was, "Well, then, I shan't keep you, Major."

He bowed, and she turned and started up the steps of the Abbey. Charles and Sara entered the chaise and, a few moments later, were on their way. "Were you able to discover their direction?" Sara asked anxiously.

"East," was the curt reply. Then, dryly, "How fortunate, for me, that I must head in that direction, in any event. If our fortune continues, perhaps I need not even miss my ship!"

Sara's eyes met his, in swift concern. "Are you so pressed for time, then?" she asked.

He nodded. "But I have no choice, have I? She *is* my sister, little though I may relish that fact, at the moment. I wish you will explain to me, though, how

Kitty could possibly do such a thing. *And* I wish you will explain what you meant when you spoke of Lord Danver's anger."

Sara quietly told him what had occurred, beginning with Lady Jersey's ball and ending with the fight at breakfast that morning. Charles listened in angry silence. When she was done, he said, "She should never have been placed in Aunt Adele's care. Your mother is a dear creature, Sara, but utterly incapable of controlling a hoyden like my sister. And so I should have advised my father, had I been consulted when this harebrained notion was hatched!"

This was too much for Sara, who retorted, "Oh? And what *would* you have advised? Kitty may be young, but I assure you it was past time she should be brought out! Do you suggest, perhaps, that your mother would have managed better? You know as well as I that she does not enjoy the best of health."

Charles met her eyes ruefully. In a different tone, he said, "I do know it. And I know that it is you have had to keep watch over my sister. Nor do I mean to chafe at *you*, for I freely admit that, in your place, I should have no notion how to manage Kitty!"

Sara laughed bitterly. "Nor have I. I begin to think our only hope is that Kitty should be laid up with some minor ailment until *someone* contrives a solution."

Charles gave a shout of genuine laughter then. "For someone who is generally so proper, Sara, you have the most outrageous mind!"

Sara could not but laugh also, at this, and feel

very much in charity with her handsome cousin. She leaned back, content to let him order their pursuit.

More than once he ordered the chaise to halt so that he might ask if Danver's travelling coach had been seen. In every case, the answer was yes, for the Earl's carriage made an impressive sight, one not quickly forgotten. As they covered the miles, Sara could not help thinking of his lordship and wondering what he would think when he discovered she was gone. Particularly as it became clear that she would *not* reach the Abbey, with Tiverton and Kitty in tow, before nightfall. Sara could only hope that he would be late, himself.

But he was not. Indeed, it was midafternoon when Lord Danver, returning to Swinford Abbey, was greeted by a rather distressed Parkins, who blurted out, "Good afternoon, my lord. It's Miss Sara, I think she's run away!"

Danver looked at his butler in astonishment. "Are you sober, Parkins?"

Parkins made an effort to be more coherent. "The gentleman came to see Miss Sara Farthingham, and she left with him, with her cloak. The gentleman asked Miss Sara if she wished to leave a message for you, and she said no, that she hoped you would merely think she was going out for a drive."

Perplexed, Danver retorted, "Surely you misunderstood, Parkins. I cannot conceive of anything more improbable. Who was the gentleman?"

Before Parkins could answer, a voice from the stairs said, "Major Charles Farthingham."

Danver turned swiftly, to see Henrietta regarding

him with serious eyes. As he watched, she descended the few remaining stairs and came over to him. Looking up, she added, "The Major was driving in a post-chaise and four, hired, I presume. He said he was taking Sara for one last drive before he left for the Continent." She hesitated, then resolutely went on, "It seemed to me, Edward, that Sara was remarkably nervous."

As she spoke, Danver went pale. "When?" he said tersely.

"No more than an hour," Parkins said hastily, "perhaps less."

"Have my curricle brought round. And the matched bays," Danver ordered curtly. "I'll leave as soon as I've changed."

"What will you do?" Henrietta said quietly.

"Find her. Strangle her. Bring her back," was the furious reply.

"But why did she go?" Henny persisted.

Danver looked at her, his face taut. "I'm afraid I may have frightened her, ma'am. Certainly I gave her little enough reason to believe I should make her an amiable husband. God grant that I have the chance to make amends!"

She nodded, then said briskly, "You'd best go change."

Fifteen minutes later, he was gone, headed east, choosing to take no one with him. Timothy protested, but was quickly sent back to the stables; Danver wanted no witnesses on this journey.

Sara and Charles, driving grimly after Tiverton and Kitty, had no notion that they, themselves, were being pursued. Nevertheless, they traveled as quickly as they could. Gradually it became clear that they were gaining on the Earl of Danver's travelling coach, until they were no more than a quarter-hour behind. It was at this point that one of the leaders cast a shoe. Sara and Charles were, perforce, required to go slowly to the nearest post house. Once there, Charles sent Sara inside while he inquired about fresh horses. "For these are nearly blown, anyway," he confided.

A few minutes later, he joined her in the private parlour. "There are no fresh horses to be had," he explained grimly, "but the smith has promised to attend to the shoe, at once." Seeing her dismay, Charles added, "We should be able to change horses at the next post house. Meanwhile, I suggest we have something to eat while we wait."

Sara would have declined, but common sense informed her that they would have a hard drive to catch the pair, and then a long drive back to Swinford Abbey, and it was not certain when she would next have a chance to eat. So she accepted. Charles was frankly relieved. But then, trust Sara to be sensible!

Finally, word was brought that the horses were ready. As Charles draped Sara's cloak over her shoulders, he said gently, "Don't worry. I assure you we shall make up the time."

She looked at him gratefully, but confessed, "I have been thinking about Lord Danver. I very much fear he is going to be angry."

Charles answered sternly, "He should have

guessed the mischief his ill-considered words would have! Had *he* been more understanding, there would have been no need for this journey. It is you who should be angry at him! In any case, he cannot blame *you!*"

"You are quite mistaken, I do blame her!" a familiar voice came from behind them.

Sara and Charles turned, as one, to see Lord Danver standing in the open doorway, his riding crop in hand. As they watched, he came closer, closing the door behind him. His eyes never left Sara, and his face was grimly white. In a curt voice he said, "Leave us, Major Farthingham; I'll speak with you later."

"No!" Charles said instantly.

Sara, her face as white as the Earl's, looked at Charles and said, "Please go, Charles. I don't understand why his lordship is so angry, but I'm not afraid of him, I promise you."

Charles hesitated, then answered, "I'll be in the coffee room."

As the door closed behind Farthingham, Danver's voice slashed through Sara like steel. "So you don't understand my anger, Miss Farthingham? I was, perhaps, supposed to accept, with complacency, your elopement with your cousin Major Farthingham? By God, you must think I've no pride at all!"

Fighting a rising tide of dizziness, Sara heard herself answer in a voice as hard as Danver's, "On the contrary, my lord! I have always felt you suffered from an *excess* of pride! Would you care to know *why* I am here, with Charles?"

His lips curled in distaste. "I know all that I need to know, so spare me the Cheltenham tragedy. I can well guess that I figure as an ogre." He paused, then laughed harshly. "You did warn me, did you not, that you would take such a step?"

Sara turned her back to him, trying to control her own temper. Danver, seeing her head bent in distress, felt an unaccountable urge to comfort her. He did not. Instead, he waited, and, eventually, she turned and faced him, her hands clasped before her. Speaking quietly, she said, "This accomplishes nothing, my lord. I must make you understand. Charles and I are not eloping." She paused, saw his start of incredulity, and stammered, "No! Not that, either!"

Danver was all icy politeness. "I suppose you will tell me that your cousin is escorting you to visit relatives? When I find you headed for the coast, and when the Major has told Henny that he is leaving for the Continent at once? Come, Sara, you'll need a better tale than that!" She could only stare at him helplessly, and he went on inexorably, "Very well, Miss Farthingham, you have accomplished your purpose. I shall send a notice, in the morning, to the papers, retracting our engagement."

As they stared at one another, both pale, the door was flung open and Kitty ran to Sara. She was followed by Sir Frederick Tiverton, who advanced far more slowly. "Sara!" Kitty cried. "Charlie says you came all this way, after *us*?"

As she nodded, Tiverton said, with an unaccustomed dignity, "You need not have, ma'am. When I guessed what Miss Katherine was about, I must have turned back."

Sara regarded him ruefully. "I wasn't certain that you *would* guess, Sir Frederick. At least, not in time."

Kitty, pouting, pulled away from Sara and said, "I left you a note, explaining! I never thought you'd try to stop me. Didn't you understand?"

Neither Sara nor Tiverton was impressed. Sternly Sara said, "You can make all the explanations you choose, tomorrow. Now, I can only wish to return to Swinford Abbey and hope that no word of this leaks out."

Quietly Tiverton said, "I'm sorry for the trouble you've been put to, ma'am. Your cousin Major Farthingham informs me that he must continue toward the coast tonight. There is ample room in our carriage, however, and I assure you we intend to return at once."

Here Danver's voice intruded icily. "Thank you, Freddy, but Sara will ride with me."

Sara met his gaze, her chin high. "I will return with Kitty and Sir Frederick."

After a long moment, his temper barely under control, Danver snapped, "Very well. I shall see you back at the Abbey."

Sara nodded, then looked at Tiverton. "Shall we go, sir?"

Tiverton nodded also. "I shall meet you downstairs in five minutes."

He and Kitty left, and Sara was alone with Lord Danver once more. Feeling a sense of panic, she would have brushed past him, but he laid a gentle hand on her arm. Sara looked at Danver coldly as she said, "I trust, my lord, you will not forget to send that notice to the papers."

"Sara!" It was a plea.

After a moment, reading the answer in her eyes, Danver released Sara's arm, and she swept out of the room. Downstairs, she found Charles waiting for her, all concern. "Sara, Tiverton tells me you are returning to the Abbey with Kitty and him? Is that what you wish?"

"I have little choice, have I?" she answered bitterly, on the verge of tears. Then, seeing his distress, she made an effort to say calmly, "Truly, Charles, I will be all right. Go on, to your ship, and don't worry about me."

Reluctantly he acceded. Just then, Sir Frederick came to tell Sara that the carriage was waiting, and she went with him, feeling Charles's concerned eyes on her back.

In the carriage, Kitty was in a contrite mood. "Charlie says that Danver is angry at you?" When Sara nodded, Kitty cried impulsively, "Oh, Sara! I never meant to cause trouble between you and Lord Danver!"

Her face partly hidden by shadows, Sara answered softly. "Fustian! It was not your fault, Kitty. Lord Danver and I . . . We made a mistake. Fortunately, we have discovered it in time."

Kitty and Tiverton were still distressed, but there was nothing more they could say. Good manners compelled them to pretend to accept her words. Feeling perilously close to tears, Sara sat stiffly erect in her corner of the coach and began making plans for a retreat. Her uncle's estate, perhaps, if only her mother (and Kitty) could be brought to see the wisdom of such a step.

Driving his curricle, close behind them, Danver was no less distressed. Cursing himself for a cow-handed fool, he considered how differently matters might have gone had he only been able to attach Sara's affection.

The two parties reached Swinford Abbey well after nightfall. All four were devoutly grateful to have reached their goal, and all four looked forward to seeking sanctuary in their rooms. Unfortunately, Lady Danver was waiting for them, flanked by Adele Farthingham and Miss Henrietta Ramsey. They stood in the entry hall, at the base of the stairs, as Parkins admitted the weary group. Caustically, Lady Danver's voice rose to slash at them. "Quite an expedition, I see! Where is your cousin, Miss Farthingham? Turned tail and fled? And you, Sir Frederick! I was never more shocked than when I learned that you and Miss Katherine Farthingham had gone off together. This must be a record for Swinford Abbey: two elopements in one day! I can only regret, Edward, that you felt the need to stop them. If it has opened your eyes, however, I must be happy that Miss Sara Farthingham showed her true colours *before* your wedding. I—"

"That's enough, Mother!" Danver's voice was soft,

but there was something in it that made Lady Danver pause. Just as quietly, he went on, "If Miss Farthingham refuses to marry me, that is *my* loss, not hers, but I have no intention of being the one to terminate the engagement!"

"Then you are a fool!" Cressilia retorted. "I have always felt so, and now you confirm my fears. I must guess that you are so besotted that if you marry her, she will lead you a fine dance!" Lady Danver cast a venomous glance at Sara, who stood beside the horrified Tiverton. "I hope you are pleased, miss! No doubt you plan to keep my son in tight leading strings? Was this elopement designed to fan his desire?"

Without thinking, Sara slowly walked forward until she stood no more than two feet away from Lady Danver. Looking down at the Countess, she said quietly, in her well-bred voice, "You give your son too little credit, ma'am, if you think he is a man to allow himself to be placed in leading strings. Or to be taken in by tricks. If you are not aware that his understanding is superior, I assure you that the rest of the world is."

"Pretty words!" Cressilia laughed contemptuously. "Then why did you elope with Major Farthingham? Don't try to deny it, for Parkins overhead you!"

Sara felt Danver move to stand beside her. Appalled, she heard herself say, "Do you often gossip with your servants, Lady Danver?"

For a moment, there was a stunned silence, and it would have been difficult to say whose face was a deeper crimson: Sara's or Cressilia's. Well, in for a penny, in for a pound, Sara thought, before adding aloud, "If you must insult your son by believing such tales, I beg you will not do so to me, for I tell you frankly, I won't tolerate it!"

Sara would have turned and walked away then, head held high, but Danver's arm, sliding around her waist, held her captive. Impossible to break free without a struggle. Looking up at him, Sara found Danver's ironic stare resting on his mother's face. Slowly, Lady Danver turned toward the stairs. Her face wooden, she spoke over her shoulder, in wounded accents. "I remove to the Dower House tomorrow."

All eyes were on Danver, but he only watched as his mother climbed the stairs, wrapped in outraged dignity. Adele would have gone to Sara, but something in the Earl's face held her back, and instead, she nodded to Kitty to follow her. Incredibly swiftly, the others melted away, as well, leaving Sara and Edward alone in the entry hall. Sara would have fled to her room, also, but Danver's arm still gripped her waist. Feeling her attempt to pull away, he said quietly, "I think not, Sara! You and I have some things to talk about."

He let go of Sara's waist, only to grab her wrist, instead. It would have been undignified to struggle, so she did not, preferring to go quietly with him, to the library. Once inside that room, Edward released her and turned to close the doors carefully. Her heart pounding now, Sara fled to the fireplace, the farthest point in the room. Danver followed slowly, making no effort to recapture her. Instead, he leaned his broad shoulders against the wall and thrust his hands into his pockets. Striving for equal calm, Sara faced him. "You wished to speak with me?" she said coolly.

He nodded, and asked, "Why didn't you tell my mother we were no longer betrothed?"

"I . . . I felt it was not her affair!" Sara retorted. "Besides, I felt it was your place to tell her, not mine." He said nothing, and she added, "Or do you mean for her to read the notice in the papers?"

Edward pushed away from the wall and came alarmingly nearer as he said, "I think—indeed, I am very sure—that the only notice in the papers will be the notice of our wedding." She would have fled, but there was nowhere to go. Danver possessed himself of both her hands and commanded rougly, "Sara, look at me!" When she did, Sara found him staring down at her in a most disturbing way. "Do you really hate me so very much?" he demanded softly.

Sara looked away, trying to free her hands. "Th-this is absurd, my lord!"

"Edward!"

"Edward," she conceded reluctantly. Rallying her pride, she began again, "A marriage in which the two people involved are indifferent to each other is repugnant to me."

"And to me!" he retorted. "But I do not believe you *are* indifferent to me. Listen, my girl, I mean to marry you, and neither your pride nor mine shall be allowed to stand in the way."

Her head still lowered, Sara said, "You were ready enough to let me go earlier."

She could feel his frown as he answered quietly, "I was in a rage, Sara. And I believed you cared nothing for me, that you abhorred me. Even so, I'm not sure I would have found it easy to let you go."

Her head came up with a snap, demanding, "Why?"

His answer was to let go of her hands and sweep Sara into his arms, as his mouth came crushing down on hers. When he finally lifted his face from hers, Edward said simply, "Because I love you. I don't, however, love that hat," he said with a frown. "Remove it!"

Sometime later, Parkins, coming to ask Lord Danver whether he wished supper to be served, was shocked to find the pair caught up in a most improper embrace. Feeling overwhelmed at this turn of events, he would have discreetly fled. Unfortunately, Danver had seen him. "Yes?" he demanded, not letting go of Sara.

Hastily Parkins stammered out his mission. Rather absently his lordship waved a hand and said, "I don't, in the slightest, care what you do about supper. Except that you may serve Sara and me in here."

"But, Edward—" she started to protest.

He stopped her by the simple expedient of a quick kiss and told her sternly, "Hush! Haven't you the proper respect for your future husband?"

"Yes, my lord," she answered demurely.

Then, noticing the scandalized Parkins still standing there, Danver said impatiently, "Well, Parkins? What are you waiting for? Haven't you ever seen anyone in love before?"

ABOUT THE AUTHOR

April Lynn Kihlstrom was born in Buffalo, New York, and graduated from Cornell University with an M.S. in Operations Research. She, her husband, and their two children enjoy traveling and have lived in Paris, Honolulu, Georgia, and New Jersey. When not writing, April Lynn Kihlstrom enjoys needlework and devotes her time to handicapped children.

Recommended Regency Romances from SIGNET

Buy them at your local

bookstore or use coupon

on next page for ordering.

More Regency Romances from SIGNET